"You're very quiet," he told her

How could Meg reply that just being in the same room with him was a secret delight? "I'm planning my weekend," she murmured instead.

"What are your plans?" Professor Culver sounded faintly bored.

"Walking the dog, gardening, shopping."

"Well, have a good weekend—such as it is." He shook his head. "Sometimes you seem too good to be true," he said with a mocking smile.

She bit back the retort that immediately sprang to her lips and cast about for a change of subject. But before she could say a word, he was suddenly beside her. His arms came swiftly around her and for the first time ever, he kissed her. "You bring out the worst in me, Meg," he said softly. "I wonder why? It's a situation that requires some thought."

His remark disturbed her. It continued to disturb her for the rest of the evening, long after he'd left.

Betty Neels is well-known for her romances set in the Netherlands, which is hardly surprising. She married a Dutchman and spent the first twelve years of their marriage living in Holland and working as a nurse. Today she and her husband make their home in a small ancient stone cottage in England's West Country, but they return to Holland often. She loves to explore tiny villages and tour privately owned homes there, in order to lend an air of authenticity to the background of her books.

Books by Betty Neels

HARLEQUIN ROMANCE

Don't miss any of our special offers. Write to us at the following address for information on our newest releases.

Harlequin Reader Service
901 Fuhrmann Blvd., P.O. Box 1397, Buffalo, NY 14240
Canadian address: P.O. Box 603,
Fort Erie, Ont. L2A 5X3

Stormy Springtime

Betty Neels

Harlequin Books

TORONTO • NEW YORK • LONDON
AMSTERDAM • PARIS • SYDNEY • HAMBURG
STOCKHOLM • ATHENS • TOKYO • MILAN

Original hardcover edition published in 1987
by Mills & Boon Limited

ISBN 0-373-02855-5

Harlequin Romance first edition August 1987

CHAPTER ONE

THE January afternoon was already darkening and a mean wind was driving rain against the windows of a room which, in its cheerful comfort, defied the evil weather outside. It was of a fair size, with a log fire blazing in its old-fashioned chimney-piece, lighted by several table lamps and furnished tastefully if somewhat shabbily. Its three occupants were seated close to the fire: three girls, sisters, deep in discussion.

'It's absolutely certain that the house will sell at once—it's got everything the estate agents like to boast about—modernised Georgian, adequate bathrooms, a tennis court—you name it, we've got it. It should fetch a good price.'

The speaker was a handsome young woman, older than the other two but still worth a second and third glance. She was very fair, with hair cut short and meticulous make-up. She was dressed expensively but without much imagination. She glanced at her two companions and went on, 'Charles says it would be downright foolish not to sell. We should each get a share ... we shall invest ours, of course, so that James and Henry will have the proper schooling ...'

The girl sitting opposite her stretched her long legs and yawned. 'Thank heaven I can please myself! I shall buy a flat near the hospital and give myself a super holiday.' She added smugly, 'I've been promised a Sister's post in a couple of months.' She was sunk in pleased thought for a few moments. 'Where will you send the boys?'

The third girl sat between them, curled up in an easy chair. She hadn't contributed to the conversation so far,

but no one had expected her to. Ever since she could
remember, she, the middle sister, had been ignored in a
kindly fashion. As a child she had been very much in
their shadows; that they were fond of her there was no
doubt, the fondness strongly mixed with kindly indifference, but from earliest childhood she had been the one
who had needed to be helped over hedges and gates, who
fell out of trees, who hung back behind her sisters when
people called. And the ease with which she passed her O
and A levels at school was quite eclipsed by their
brilliance at sports and theatricals. Besides, she was
small and plump, with a face which was only redeemed
from plainness by large grey eyes, heavily fringed, and a
wide, gentle mouth. And now, with Cora married to a
young accountant with ambition and the mother of two
small sons, and Doreen embarked on a career in
hospital—but only until such time as she could catch the
eye of some eminent doctor—she had to admit to herself
that she had nothing much to show for the last few years.
True, she had stayed at home, largely because everyone
took it for granted that she wanted to do so, and she had
looked after her mother and after a year, she had taken
over the housekeeping as well. She had, of necessity,
become an excellent cook and a splendid housewife,
helped by Betsy, who should have retired years ago but
stubbornly refused, and by Mrs Griffiths, who popped in
three times a week to do the rough work.

But now their mother was dead, her pension no longer
paid, and there was precious little money save what their
home would fetch. Cora and Doreen had never bothered
overmuch about the pension—they had taken it for
granted that it was enough for their mother and Meg to
live on and pay their way. In their fashion they had been
generous—dressing gowns and slippers and hampers at
Christmas—but neither of them had suggested that Meg
might like a holiday or even an evening out at a theatre

... Meg bore them no grudge; Cora had her own life to lead and her own home and family, and besides, she lived in Kent and came home but rarely. And as for Doreen, everyone who knew her said what a splendid nurse she was and what a brilliant future she had before her. Besides, being such a handsome young woman, she could pick and choose from among her men friends and their invitations to dine and dance and go to the theatre, which left her little time to go to Hertfordshire.

Meg had been content enough; Hertingfordbury, where they had lived all their lives, was a charming village, the main roads bypassing it so that it was left in comparative peace with its church standing in the steep churchyard, its pub, the White Horse, still doing good business since the sixteenth century, and the equally ancient cottages. There were larger houses too—Georgian, built of rose brick, standing in roomy grounds, well cared for, handed on from one generation to the next. Meg's home was perhaps not as well cared for as other similar houses—there hadn't been the money during the last few years—but she had kept the garden in good order, and even if the outside paintwork wasn't as fresh as she might wish, she had done wonders with the lofty, well-proportioned rooms. Her sisters had good-naturedly dismissed her hours of careful painting and wallpapering as a pleasant little hobby to keep her occupied—to their credit, they had never realised that she had enough to occupy her without any hobbies. Their mother had had a worsening heart condition which, for the last few months of her life, had confined her to bed and couch, which meant a good deal of running to and fro and disturbed nights for Meg. And Meg, being Meg, had never complained. Not that she had ever felt downtrodden or put upon; she was a girl of common sense, and it was obvious to her that, since Cora had a home and family to look after, and Doreen had set her ambitious sights on becoming the wife of some eminent doctor, it was perfectly natural for them to pursue their own interests, since she had never exhibited any ambitions of her own.

She had those, of course, hidden away deep inside her—to marry and have a home of her own, a clutch of children, animals around the place and a garden—and a husband, of course. She was a little vague about him, but he would have to love her dearly for ever ... At the moment, at any rate, there was no likelihood of meeting him. She had friends enough in the village, mostly elderly, and the young men she had grown up with had either got married or were engaged; besides, she had had very little time for the leisurely pursuits of her friends, and now that she was alone with time on her hands, she felt disinclined to join the activities in the village. Mrs Collins had died two months previously and Meg missed her sorely, more so because she had nursed her so devotedly for so long. She had gone on living alone save for Betsy, polishing the furniture, doing the flowers, tending the garden, taking it for granted that she would go on doing that for the foreseeable future. After all, it was her home, somewhere for Doreen to come when she wanted to, somewhere for Cora to send the boys to during the school holidays. She had a small annuity from her grandmother, just enough to live on and to pay Betsy and Mrs Griffiths.

She sat quietly now, filled with cold surprise and uncertainty. When Cora had finished explaining where the boys were to go to school, she asked, 'What about me—and Betsy?'

They turned to look at her, smiling reassuringly. 'Why, darling, you'll have your share, enough to buy a little flat somewhere—you could get a job—you'd like that after the quiet life you've been leading.'

It would be a waste of breath to ask what job; she wasn't trained for anything and it was a bit late to start at twenty-three. 'And Betsy?'

'Remember there was something in the will about those shares Mother had? They were for Betsy. They'll top up her state pension nicely.'

'Where will she live?'

Doreen said lightly, 'There must be any number of people in the village who'd be glad to let her have a room—she knows everyone for miles around.'

She got up and sat on the edge of Meg's chair and flung an arm around her shoulders. 'I'll get everyone looking for a flat for you, darling. You'll love London, and you'll make heaps of friends. You must be lonely here in this big place.'

Meg said in a wooden voice, 'No. I miss Mother, but it's still home, and there's plenty to keep me busy—and the garden even in winter.'

'We'll find you a basement flat with a paved area; you can fill it with pot plants.'

Meg let that pass. She said in her matter-of-fact way, 'I'll have to train for something,' and then, 'I suppose I *have* to leave here?' Neither of her sisters heard the wistfulness in her voice.

'Shorthand and typing,' said Cora, '—jobs going all the time for shorthand typists . . .'

'Receptionist?' suggested Doreen vaguely. She didn't say what for. 'Anyway, that's settled, isn't it? Let's get the estate agents on to it, Cora—there's a flat near the hospital which I rather like. There is no point in waiting, is there?'

'What about the furniture?' Meg had a quiet voice, but it brought them up short.

'Sell it?' essayed Cora.

'Put it in store? I could use it—some of it—in my new flat when I get it.'

Meg said slowly, 'Why not sell it with the house?' At the back of her mind there was an idea taking slow shape. She wasn't quite sure of it at the moment, but it would need thinking about later.

Cora looked at her approvingly. 'That's not a bad idea. We'll see what the agents say. I must fly—the boys will be back and Natasha—the au pair—is no good at all. I'll have to find someone else.'

They kissed Meg goodbye, went out to their cars, and got in and drove away, and Meg went back into the house and sat down in the gathering gloom to think. If it were humanly possible, she didn't intend to leave her home, and certainly not to leave old Betsy to live out her days in a poky bedsitter. Presently Betsy came in with the tea-tray and Silky, the rather battered tomcat Meg had found skulking round the back door, had fed and sheltered and, since he had obviously made up his mind to become one of the family, had adopted. He got on to Meg's lap now, and Betsy put the tray down and said, 'Well, they've gone, then?' There was a question mark behind the words which couldn't be ignored.

'Cora and Doreen want to sell the house,' said Meg. 'And everything in it. But don't worry, Betsy, I've an idea . . . so that we can stay here.'

'Marry a millionaire, like as not, Miss Meg.' Betsy's cockney voice sounded cheerfully derisive. 'What's to happen to us, then?'

Meg said hearteningly, 'It takes weeks—months—to sell a house. I'll do something about it, I promise you.'

Betsy was only too willingly reassured; she trotted back to the kitchen and Meg sat drinking her tea, thinking about the future. Of course it would be marvellous if a very rich man came along and bought the house and fell in love with her at the same time, but that only happened in books . . . What was needed was someone elderly who needed a housekeeper or companion and a good plain cook and who didn't object to an elderly tomcat. Meg, who was a practical girl, thought it unlikely, though there was no harm in hoping.

Her sisters wasted no time. Within a week a pleasant young man from a London estate agent came to inspect the property. He walked round, with Meg beside him explaining about the old-fashioned bathrooms, the central heating, the Aga stove and why the large drawing-room was icy cold.

'There's only me,' she pointed out, 'there's no point in having a fire there just for one—my sisters are seldom here. We switch on the central heating twice a week, though, because of the furniture—Hepplewhite, you know.'

He nodded, rather at sea; he knew a lot about houses but not much about furniture. He felt vaguely sorry for the rather mouselike girl who was showing him round with such a self-possessed air. He spared a moment to wonder where she would go when the house was sold, for sold it would be, he could see that. Fine old Georgian houses with a generous spread of garden were much sought after. He accepted the coffee she offered him, agreed with her that people wishing to view the house might do so only with an appointment, and took his leave.

The first couple came within three days. In the morning, because Meg was on the committee which organised the Church Bazaar and that would take the whole afternoon.

Mr and Mrs Thorngood arrived in a splendid Mercedes and Meg, rarely given to criticising anyone, disliked them on sight. She led them round her home, listening with a calm face to their loud-voiced remarks about old-fashioned bathrooms, no fitted cupboards and a kitchen which must have come out of the Ark. They didn't like the garden, either: no swimming pool, all those trees and outbuildings which were of no use to anyone . . .

'We use the end one as a garage,' Meg pointed out.

'Well, that wouldn't do for us—we've three cars—we'd need to build a decent garage.' The man looked at her angrily as though it were her fault, and presently the pair of them drove away.

The next day a middle-aged woman with an overbearing manner came. She was looking for suitable premises for a school, she explained, but it took her only a short time to decide that the house wouldn't do at all. 'Most unsuitable,' she observed to Meg, who was politely standing on the doorstep to see her off. 'All those plastered ceilings, and none of the bedrooms would take more than five beds.'

Meg liked the next couple. They were young and friendly and admired everything wholeheartedly. It wasn't until they were drinking coffee with her in the sitting-room that the girl said suddenly, 'We can't possibly buy this place; actually we live in a poky little flat in Fulham, but when Mike's between jobs, we go around inspecting houses—it's fun, seeing how the other half live. I hope you don't mind.' She sighed. 'It must be nice to be rich and live in a lovely old house like this one.'

'Well', began Meg and decided not to go on. 'I'm glad you like it, anyway. It's been in the family for a fairly long time.'

There were quite a few viewers during the next week, but none of them came back a second time, although one man made an offer of slightly less than the price the agents had set. Instantly rejected, of course.

Then no one came at all for four days. Meg breathed a sigh of relief; perhaps no one would want to live in her home and she would be able to stay on there. She knew it was silly to think that; she would have to go sooner or later to some tiny basement flat unless she could find something to do locally. That wouldn't be easy, since she had no skills.

As each day passed she felt more and more lulled into false hopes; she ceased listening for the phone, put in hours of work in the garden and went for long walks. The weather had turned nasty—perhaps that was why no one came, but it made no difference to her. On the afternoon of the fourth day she came home from a muddy wet walk, kicked her sensible boots off at the back door and was met by an agitated Betsy.

'There's a gentleman,' said the old lady, all agog. 'The estate agent rang just after you'd gone and said he was on his way. I had to let him in . . . He's in the drawing-room.'

'Is he now? Well, he'll have to wait a bit longer, won't he, while I get tidied up? Bother the man!'

She had sat down on the floor of the back lobby, the better to pull off the old socks she wore inside her boots, and at a kind of gulping sound from Betsy, she turned her head. There was a man standing in the lobby doorway. A towering, wide-shouldered giant with black hair and even blacker eyes. Very good-looking too, thought Meg, and frowned fiercely at him. He had her at a disadvantage, and the nasty little smile on his thin mouth made that apparent.

'I must apologise,' he said in a voice which held no apology at all, and waited for her to speak. She sat there looking up at him. There was not much point in getting up until she had the socks off; for one thing she guessed that he must be over six feet and she was a mere five foot three; he would still look down on her. She disposed of the socks, stood up and pushed her feet into a shabby pair of slippers and flung off her wet raincoat, dragged off the scarf she had tied round her hair and addressed him coolly. 'No need,' she told him. 'You weren't to know that I wasn't at home.' She tossed back her damp hair, hanging untidily round her damp face, rosy from the wind and rain. 'You would like to see round the house?'

'You are right, that was my object in coming,' he informed her.

Oh, very stuffy, decided Meg, and led the way to the front hall which was, after all, the starting point. She had the patter off by heart now: the Adam fireplace in the drawing-room, the strap work on the dining-room ceiling, the rather special Serpentine scroll balustrade on the staircase, and as they wandered in and out of the bedrooms on the first floor she pointed out the quite ugly cast-iron fireplace—writhing forms, a mid-Victorian addition which her companion pronounced in a cold voice as frankly hideous. But other than that, he had little to say. She thought it very likely that the sight of the old-fashioned bathrooms with pipes all over the place and great cast-iron baths sitting on clawed feet in the middle of the rooms left him bereft of words. She was quite sure that it was a waste of time taking him round; she took his final comment—'A most interesting house'—as a polite way of getting himself out of the door. Not that she considered him a polite man; he should have stayed where Betsy put him, in the drawing-room, until he could have been fetched at the proper time and with suitable dignity.

She stood with him on the steps outside the front door, waiting for him to go. Only he didn't. 'You live here alone?' he asked.

'No—Betsy lives here with me.'

He glanced at her ringless, rather grubby hands. For a moment she thought that he was going to say something more, but he didn't. His, 'Thank you, Miss Collins,' was brisk and impersonal as he trod down the steps and got into the dark grey Rolls-Royce parked on the sweep before the house. He didn't look round either, but drove away without so much as a backward glance.

''andsome man,' remarked Betsy, coming into the hall

as Meg closed the door. 'Nicely spoken, too. P'raps 'e'll buy . . .'

Meg said quite vehemently, 'I found him a rude man, and I hope never to see him again, Betsy.' Whereupon she flew upstairs and took a good look at herself in the pier glass in what had been her mother's room. Her reflection hardly reassured her; her nose shone, her hair was still damp and wispy and the serviceable guernsey and elderly tweed skirt she wore when she was gardening hardly enhanced her appearance. The slippers completed a decidedly unfashionable appearance. She wondered what he had thought of her, and then forgot him; he had joined all the house-hunters whom she would never see again. She wasn't even sure of his name—he had given it to her, but she hadn't paid attention. She could, of course, have asked Betsy, but she didn't; for some reason she wanted to forget him.

January slipped away into February and it turned cold and snowed. Cora and Doreen phoned each week, wanting to know if anyone had made a bid for the house and giving excellent reasons why they couldn't get down to see her. Meg, accepting them without rancour, none the less wished for more sisterly support. She was happy as things were, but there all the time at the back of her mind was the thought that sooner or later she would have to give up her home and live in some poky flat in an endless row of equally poky flats . . . Indeed, Doreen had told her only the evening before that she had heard of a semi-basement on the fringes of Highgate; two rooms and bathroom and kitchen—there wouldn't be much money over by the time Meg had bought it with her share, but then Meg would get a job easily enough.

'What at?' asked Meg of Betsy, who shook her head and said nothing at all.

No one could come until the snow had gone. Meg pottered round the house, polished the silver and got in

Betsy's way in the kitchen. It was something of a shock when the estate agents phoned to say that there was a Mrs Culver on her way.

Meg, who had been in the kitchen making marmalade with Betsy, went to her room and tidied herself, re-did her hair, ran a powder puff over her face, changed into the cashmere sweater she kept for special occasions, and went downstairs just in time to watch an elderly but beautifully kept Daimler draw up before the door. She skipped into the drawing-room and picked up a book; it would never do to be caught snooping.

The doorbell rang and Betsy, in a clean apron, but smelling delightfully of marmalade on the boil, answered it and presently ushered Mrs Culver into the room.

'You're making marmalade,' observed that lady as she advanced across the wide expanse of Moorfields carpet. 'One of the most delightful aromas there is.' She smiled at Meg. 'How do you do? You will be Miss Collins? You must forgive me for coming at such an awkward time and at such short notice; I am only just back in England.'

Meg murmured politely; she hadn't met anyone like Mrs Culver before. She was a small, rather plump woman, well into middle age, but so well dressed and exquisitely made-up that she gave the lie to that. Not pretty but with a delightful smile and twinkling eyes so that one was forced to smile back at her.

'It's quite convenient,' Meg assured her. 'Would you like to sit and rest for a few minutes or would you like to look round now?'

'May I look round?' Mrs Culver studied her surroundings. 'This is a charming room.'

Meg found herself liking the little lady. She led the way back into the hall and started her tour, and found for once an appreciative companion. What was more, Mrs Culver didn't seem at all put off by the bathroom pipes, and remarked upon the elegance of the Adam fireplace before Meg could even mention it.

'I like this house,' observed Mrs Culver as they returned to the drawing-room. 'I shall buy it.'

Meg said rather faintly, 'Oh, will you? Would you like some coffee?'

'Indeed I would,' and when Meg returned from the kitchen, 'Tell me, has it been in your family for a long time?'

'Ages. It was built in 1810, but of course it's had things done to it since then.'

'But not very recently,' remarked Mrs Culver drily, 'therein lies its charm. I promise you that if I do do anything at all it will be done so well that you wouldn't even notice it.'

Meg poured the coffee, wrestling with a variety of feelings. It was splendid news for Cora and Doreen, of course, but not for her and Betsy. The poky flat loomed large, and how was she going to bear leaving her home? She stifled these feelings with the common sense she had cultivated since she was a child; the house had to be sold, and who better to buy it than this nice elderly lady who liked the making of marmalade and knew an Adam fireplace when she saw one? She said, 'You'll be very happy here,' and meant it. 'Do you want the name of our solicitor or would you like to think about it first?'

'I've thought, my dear. I shall go straight to the estate agents and then instruct my solicitor.' She paused and frowned. 'There is just one thing.'

Meg waited for Mrs Culver to go on. Problems sometimes turned into insurmountable snags—it would be the bathrooms and those pipes. She herself had grown up with them, but every single person who had inspected the house had remarked upon them. She assumed a sympathetically listening face and looked across at her companion.

'My housekeeper,' began that lady, 'has been waiting

for some months for an operation—something to do with her toes—and only this morning she told me that there was a bed for her at last. She offered to put the whole thing off, bless her, until it was convenient for me, but I can't have that—it isn't an emergency, you understand, but it will take time before she can come back to me— nasty little pins in her toes to straighten them, so I'm told, and when she does return she must have someone to do the lion's share of the work until she can cope once again. I'm told that when she has got over whatever it is that they intend to do to her, her feet will be like new. She has been with me for more than twenty years and is a treasure as well as a friend.' She stopped to take a breath. 'Very like that nice woman who opened the door to me.'

'Betsy—she's been with me since I was a baby.'

Mrs Culver eyed Meg thoughtfully. 'It's scarcely my business to ask, but when you leave here, will she go with you? If not, would she consider staying on until my Kate is well enough again? Two months at least ... and I suppose you wouldn't know of a good cook? Someone to work with her—it's a big house and I'm not allowed to be energetic. I dare say I could get someone from the village to help with the rough work.' She smiled at Meg. 'I'm an impertinent old woman, aren't I? And you're at liberty to say so if you wish.'

'I wouldn't dream of it, and I don't think you are anyway,' declared Meg. 'It's a most sensible idea. As a matter of fact, my sisters want me to go and live in London in a flat and find a job, and they thought Betsy could find a room in the village.' She felt a strong urge to tell Mrs Culver all about her sisters' arrangements and plans, but of course that was out of the question.

Mrs Culver nodded and gave Meg a sharp glance, sensing that there was a lot left unsaid. 'What work will you do?' she asked.

'I have no idea. I'm not trained for anything; our

mother was ill for a long time so I took over the housekeeping, and Betsy taught me to cook ...' She stopped suddenly and stared at her companion, who stared back.

'It's as plain as the nose on my face,' said Mrs Culver. 'I suspect that we're being unbusinesslike and impulsive, but I've always relied on my female intuition, and it tells me that I can't go wrong. Will you stay on as housekeeper and have your Betsy to help you? It would give you time to settle your future; I dare say you're in no hurry to go and live in a London flat. And dear old Kate can have her feet put right without worrying about getting back to me until she's quite fit and well. Would you mind being a housekeeper, my dear?'

Meg hadn't felt so happy for months; the dreaded London flat could be abrogated at least for a month or two, she could stay in her home, doing exactly what she had been doing for some years, and Betsy would have time to get used to changes. Her vague idea had become reality.

'I wouldn't mind at all, Mrs Culver. I'd like it very much and I know Betsy would too, and if you want someone for the rough work, Mrs Griffiths, the postman's wife, has been coming here for years.'

They beamed at each other, and Mrs Culver asked, 'The garden? Is there a man ...?'

'Well, no, I've been doing the gardening, though you could do with someone for the hedges and the digging—I've had to leave a good bit.'

'Well, you find someone, my dear; I'm sure I can safely leave it to you—and more help in the house if you need it. I suppose it will take the solicitors weeks to get things settled—I've been mystified as to why. But in the meantime, will you go on as you have been doing? I'll write to you as soon as things are settled, and we must have a talk before I move in.' She looked round the pleasant room. 'Would you consider selling the furniture? There must be treasured pieces you would want to keep so that you can furnish your flat eventually, but the rest?'

'I'll have to ask my sisters,' said Meg. 'They did suggest that I had some of it and my younger sister might want some things—she hopes to buy a flat near the hospital and live out.'

'And you have another sister?'

'Yes, older than me—she's married and doesn't want anything here.'

Mrs Culver got up to go. 'Well, we can settle that when you have seen them, can't we? You're sure that you are happy about our little arrangement?'

Meg smiled widely. 'Oh, yes—very happy. I—I really am not too keen on living in London.' They walked unhurriedly to the door, pleased with each other's company. 'Would you like a word with Betsy?'

'A very good idea. Shall we go to the kitchen, if she's there?'

Betsy's elderly face crumpled into dozens of wrinkles at the news; she looked as though she might cry, but she chuckled instead. 'There, Miss Meg—yer never know, do yer? What's round the corner, I mean. I'm sure I'll bide 'ere and 'appy ter do so just as long as I'm needed.'

'I'm so glad,' said Mrs Culver, and shook Betsy's hand. 'I look forward to living here in this nice old house.'

Meg saw her out to the car and gave the solid-looking man who opened the car door a guilty look. He understood at once. 'Your cook kindly gave me a coffee, miss,' he told her. 'Thank you.'

'Oh, good—I'm sorry I forgot—as long as Betsy saw to your comfort.'

She put her head through the still-open door. 'I'm glad it's you,' she told Mrs Culver, who was being cosily tucked in with rugs by the chauffeur. 'Mother and Father would have liked to have met you.'

'Why, thank you, my dear—what a nice thing to say. You shall hear from me very shortly. Goodbye.'

Over their midday snack Meg and Betsy talked over the morning. They found it difficult to believe that it had all happened. 'It's like a fairy tale,' said Meg. 'I can't believe it . . . I know it's not going to last, but it does give us another month or so. We'll be here when the daffodils are out.' She cut a wedge of cheese. 'You're to have your wages, Betsy, and so am I—nice to be paid for something I've been doing for nothing for years!'

She fell silent, her busy mind exploring the chances of getting a job as housekeeper when she finally left—if Mrs Culver would give her a reference she might be lucky—then there would be no need to live in London. Presently she said, 'I must let Cora and Doreen know,' and went to the telephone in what had been her father's study.

Of course they were both delighted.

'Now we can get the boys' names down for school,' said Cora.

'I'll make a firm offer for that flat,' Doreen decided and added as an afterthought, 'once it's all dealt with, Meg, I'll look out for something for you —you'd better take a course in shorthand and typing.'

It seemed hardly the time to tell them that Mrs Culver had plans of her own; Meg put down the receiver without having said a word about herself and Betsy, but then, neither of them had asked.

There was purpose in the days now: the house to clean and polish, cupboards to turn out, the silver to polish, wrap up and stow away, curtains to be cleaned . . . Mrs Griffiths, when approached, was glad enough to continue coming three times a week, and what was more, she had an out-of-work nephew who would be glad to see to the garden.

There were letters too, learned ones from the solicitor,

triumphant ones from the estate agents and a steady flow of instructions from Cora and Doreen. What was more important was that there was a letter from Mrs Culver, stating that she would be glad to employ both Meg and Betsy, and setting out their wages in black and white. She had urged the solicitors to make haste, she had written, and hoped to move in in about three weeks' time.

'A nice letter,' said Meg, putting it back neatly into its envelope. 'I wonder where I've heard the name Culver before?'

She discovered the very next day. It was a lovely day, clear and frosty and with a brief sunshine which held no warmth but gave the illusion of spring. She was perched on a window-seat in the drawing-room, carefully mending one of the old, but still beautiful, brocade curtains, when a car drew up and a man got out. She remembered him at once—who could forget him, being the size and height he was anyway? She watched him walk unhurriedly to the door and pull the old-fashioned bell, and then listened to Betsy's feet trotting across the hall to open the door.

If he had had second thoughts, decided Meg with satisfaction, he was going to be disappointed. She remembered the look he had given the bathroom pipes and the Victorian fireplace; he would make an offer, perhaps, far below the one asked, and she would find great satisfaction in refusing it.

It wasn't like that at all. Betsy ushered him in. 'Mr Culver to see you, Miss Meg.' She winked as she went out.

Meg got up and said uncertainly, 'Have you come about the house? It's sold——' and at the same instant said, 'Culver—you aren't by any chance related to Mrs Culver?'

'Her son. I suggested that she should come and see the place; I knew she'd like it.' He raised dark eyebrows.

'You're disconcerted, Miss Collins?'

Meg eyed him cautiously, for he sounded cross. 'Not that,' she explained politely, 'just surprised. I'd forgotten your name, you see.'

'You're to remain here as my mother's housekeeper? Oh, don't look alarmed—I have no intention of interfering with her plans. It seems a most suitable arrangement. But you do understand that when Kate, her own housekeeper, returns, you and your servant will have to go.'

'Betsy isn't a servant,' said Meg clearly, 'she's been with my family for a very long time. She's our friend and helper.'

The eyebrows rose once more. 'I stand corrected! May I sit down?'

She flushed. 'I'm sorry, please do. Why have you come, Mr Culver? And you had no need to remind me that we're only here temporarily.'

'I came to tell you that within the week there will be some furniture delivered, and to ask you to remove whatever you wish to keep for yourself. Presumably there are attics?'

'Three large ones, and yes, I'll do that.'

'A cheque for the furniture, which will be valued, will be paid to your solicitor in due course. Tell me, Miss Collins, don't your sisters want to discuss this with you?'

'No—my elder sister is married and my younger sister is too busy—she's a staff nurse in London . . .'

'And you?' For once his voice was friendly, and she responded to it without thinking.

'Me? I can't do anything except look after a house and cook; that's why I'm so happy to stay on here for a little while.'

She studied his bland face for a while. 'You don't mind?' she asked.

'Why should I mind?' He got to his feet. 'I won't keep

you any longer. Let your solicitor know if there's anything which worries you.'

Meg went with him to the door, and because he looked somehow put out about something, she said gently, 'I'm sorry you don't like me staying here, Mr Culver, but it won't be for long.'

He took her hand in his. 'That's what I'm afraid of, Miss Collins,' he told her gravely. 'Goodbye.'

CHAPTER TWO

MEG shut the door firmly behind Mr Culver and then stood looking at the painted panelling in the hall. She wondered what he had meant; it was a strange remark to make, and it made no sense. She dismissed it from her mind and wandered off to the kitchen to tell Betsy about the furniture. 'So we'd better go round the house and pick out what we want,' she ended. 'I'll try and get Doreen to come down and sort out what she wants.'

Doreen came two days later, full of plans for herself and for Meg. 'You'll have to go into a bedsitter or digs for a while,' she told her. 'I'll ask around . . .'

'There's no need; I'm staying on here as housekeeper, and Betsy's staying too,' she said, and before an astonished Doreen could utter a word, added, 'I'll explain.'

When she had finished, Doreen said, 'Well, I don't know—housekeeper in your own home—it's a bit demeaning, and such hard work!'

'But I've been housekeeping for years,' Meg pointed out, 'and besides, I'm going to be paid for it now.'

Doreen was a bit huffy; she had been telling Meg what to do and how to do it since they were children, and until now Meg had meekly followed her lead. 'Oh, well,' she said grudgingly, 'I suppose you know your own mind best, though I think it's a mistake. Cora won't like it . . .'

'Why not?' asked Meg placidly. 'I should have thought you'd have both been pleased that I'm settled for a month or two.' She added cunningly, 'You'll be able to concentrate on your new flat.'

A remark which caused her sister to subside, still grumbling but resigned. Moreover, she declared that she would be down the following weekend to choose furniture. 'I don't want much,' she said. 'I'm going to buy very simple modern stuff.' She added, 'Cora doesn't want anything, only those paintings of the ancestors in the hall and the silver tea and coffee sets.'

As she got into her car she asked carelessly, 'What's this son like?'

Meg paused to think. 'Well, he's very tall—about six feet four inches—and broad. He's dark and his eyes look black, though I don't suppose they are ... he's—he's arrogant and—off-hand.'

Doreen gave her a kindly, pitying look. 'Out of your depth, were you?' she asked. 'He sounds quite a dish.' She started the engine. 'What does he do?'

Meg stared at her. 'I haven't the faintest idea. We only talked about the house and the furniture.'

Doreen grinned. 'I can well believe that! When I've settled you in that semi-basement, Meg, I'm going to find you an unambitious curate.'

She shot away, and instead of going indoors Meg wandered along the path which circumvented the house. She had no wish to marry a curate, she was certain on that point, nor did she want to marry a man like her brother-in-law—something in the city and rising fast, and already pompous. She would like to marry, of course, but although she had a very clear idea of the home she would like and the children in it, not to mention dogs and cats and a donkey and perhaps a pony, the man who would provide her with all this was a vague nonentity. But she wanted to be loved and cherished, she was sure of that.

She went back into the house and sat at the kitchen table eating the little cakes Betsy had made for tea and which Doreen hadn't eaten because of her figure. 'Do you suppose I could have the furniture in my room, Betsy?' she asked at length. 'I could put a few chairs and tables in there before Mrs Culver comes, then it would be easy when we move out. I won't need much in a small flat . . .'

Betsy was beating eggs. 'Likely not,' she agreed. 'Poky places they are, them semi-basements—lived in one myself 'fore I came to yer ma. Can't see why yer 'ave ter live in one, meself.'

Meg ate another cake. 'No—well, I've been thinking. If I can get Mrs Culver to give us good references we might try for jobs in some large country house, the pair of us. I was looking through the advertisements in *The Lady*, Betsy, and there are dozens of jobs.'

'Yer ma and pa would turn in their graves if yer was ter to do that, Miss Meg—housework indeed—and you a lady born and bred. I never 'eard such nonsense!'

Meg got up and flung an arm round her old friend's shoulders. 'I think I'd rather do anything than live in a basement flat in London,' she declared. 'Let's go round the house and choose what I'll take with me.'

Small pieces for the most part: her mother's papier mâché work table, encrusted with mother-of-pearl and inlaid with metal foil, a serpentine table in mahogany with a pierced gallery, and a Martha Washington chair reputed to be Chippendale and lastly a little rosewood desk where her mother had been in the habit of writing her letters. She added two standard chairs with sabre legs, very early nineteenth century, and a sofa table on capstan base with splayed feet which went very well with the chairs and wouldn't take up too much room.

They went back to the kitchen and Meg made a neat list. 'And now you, Betsy; of course you'll have the furniture which is already in your room, but you'll need some bits and pieces.'

So they went round again, adding a rather shabby armchair Betsy had always liked, and the small, stoutly built wooden table in the scullery with its two equally stout chairs. Meg added a bookcase standing neglected in one of the many small rooms at the back of the house, and a standard lamp which had been by the bookcase for as long as she could remember. No one was going to miss it, and it would please Betsy mightily.

She got the butcher's boy from the village to come up to the house and move the furniture into her and Betsy's rooms. Doreen would see to her own things once she had chosen them.

This was something which she did at the end of the week, arriving at the house a bare five minutes after Mr Culver's second totally unexpected visit. Getting no answer from the front doorbell, he had wandered round the house and found Meg in an old sweater and slacks covered by a sacking apron, intent on arranging seed potatoes on the shelves of the potting shed. She turned to see who it was as he trod towards her, and said, rather crossly, 'Oh, it's you—you didn't say you were coming!'

He ignored that. 'It's careless of you to leave your front door open when you're not in the house, Miss Collins. You should be more careful.'

She gave him a long, considered look. He doubtless meant to be helpful, but it seemed that each time they met he said something to annoy her.

'This isn't London,' she said with some asperity, and then added in a kindly tone, 'though I dare say you mean well.'

He stood looking down his handsome nose at her. 'Naturally I have an interest in this house . . .'

'Premature,' Meg observed matter-of-factly. 'I haven't—that is, we haven't sold it to your mother yet.'

She wished the words unsaid at once: supposing that he took umbrage and advised his mother to withdraw from the sale? What would her sisters say? And she would have to start all over again, and next time she might not be as lucky as regards her future. She met his eyes and saw that he was smiling nastily.

'Exactly, Miss Collins, it behoves you to mind your words, does it not?' He added unwillingly, 'Your face is like an open book—you must learn to conceal your thoughts before you embark on a career in London!'

He looked over his shoulder as he spoke, in time to see Doreen coming towards them, and Meg, watching him, saw that he was impressed. Her sister was looking particularly pretty in a wide tweed coat, draped dramatically over her shoulders, allowing a glimpse of a narrow cashmere dress in a blue to match her eyes. She fetched up beside him, cast him a smiling glance and said, 'Hello, Meg—darling, must you root around like a farm labourer?' She peered at the potatoes. 'Such a dirty job!'

Meg said 'Hello,' and waved a grubby hand at Mr Culver. 'This is Mr Culver, Mrs Culver's son—my sister, Doreen; she's come to choose her furniture before the valuers get here.'

Mr Culver, it seemed, could make himself very agreeable if he so wished, and Doreen, of course, had always been considered a charming girl. They fell at once into the kind of light talk which Meg had never learnt to master. She carefully arranged another row of potatoes, listening admiringly to Doreen's witty chatter, and when there was a pause asked, 'Why did you come, Mr Culver?'

Not the happiest way of putting it—Doreen's look told her that—so she added, 'Is there anything we can do.'

He glanced between the pair of them, and Meg caught

the glance. Wondering how on earth we could possibly be sisters, she thought, and suddenly wished that she wasn't plain and could talk like Doreen.

'My mother asked me to call in—I'm on my way home and it isn't out of my way. She wants you to order coal and logs—a ton of each, I would suggest—and also, if you know of a young boy who would do odd jobs, would you hire him?'

'What to do?' asked Meg, ever practical. 'Not full time, I imagine?'

'I believe she was thinking of someone to carry in coal and so on. Perhaps on his way to school, or in the afternoon . . .'

'Well, there's Willy Wright—he's fifteen and looking for work. He goes to school still, but I dare say he'd be glad of the money.'

Mr Culver nodded carelessly. 'I'll leave it in your capable hands.'

'Oh, she's capable all right, our Meg,' put in Doreen. 'Always has been. You live near here, Mr Culver?' She was at her most charming.

He gave the kind of answer Meg would have expected of him. 'I work in London for most of the time. And you?'

Doreen told him, making the telling amusing and self-effacing at the same time. 'Come into the house and have a cup of tea—I know Meg is dying for us to go so that she can finish her potatoes.' She smiled at her sister. 'Finished in ten minutes or so, Meg? I'll have the tea made.'

She led the way back to the house, leaving Meg in the potting shed, quite happy to be left on her own once more. Doreen had never made a secret of the fact that she intended to marry and marry well. She thought it very likely that before Mr Culver left Doreen would have found out what he did, whether he was engaged or even married, and where he lived. She chuckled as she started on the last row of potatoes; Mr Culver had met his match.

It was half an hour before she joined them in the sitting-room, wearing a neat shirt blouse and a pleated skirt, her small waist cinched by a wide soft leather belt. Mr Culver was on the point of going, which was what she had been hoping; anyway, she wished him a coolly polite goodbye, leaving Doreen to see him to the door, assuring him that she would do as Mrs Culver asked. The moment they were in the hall, she picked up the tea-tray and whisked herself off to the kitchen to make a fresh pot. Doreen would want another cup before she started on the furniture.

'What a man!' observed that young lady as she sank into a chair. 'Is that fresh tea? I could do with a cup. Believe it or not, Meg, I couldn't get a thing out of him— he's a real charmer, no doubt of that, but as close as an oyster. I bet he's not married.' She took the cup Meg was offering. 'I wonder what he does? Perhaps you can find out . . .?'

'Why?' Meg sounded reasonable. 'He's nothing to do with us; we're not likely to see him—he only called with a message.'

Doreen looked thoughtful. 'Yes, well, we'll see. That's a nice car, and unless I'm very mistaken, his shoes are hand-made . . .'

'Perhaps he's got awkward feet,' suggested Meg, quite seriously.

Doreen looked at her to see if she was joking and saw that she wasn't, so she didn't reply. 'When's Mrs Culver due to arrive?' she asked instead. 'I'd better decide on the things I want and get them away. Have you got yours?'

Meg nodded. 'Yes, I got Willy to come up and move them. Most of it's in my room; the rest is in the attic.

Betsy's got some bits and pieces, too—in her room and some in the attic.'

'Well, I'll get it over with and have it taken up to town and stored until I want it. Does Mrs Culver want everything else? How much will she pay for it?'

'I've no idea. There's a valuer coming . . . I'll let you know as soon as he's been and she's agreed to his estimate.'

Doreen wandered off and came back presently with a scribbled list. Mostly portraits, a rent table which wouldn't really be missed in the drawing-room, a little button-backed Victorian chair from one of the bedrooms and a corner cupboard. 'Not much,' she commented. 'I'd rather have the money, anyway. Cora and I don't really like the idea of you staying on here as housekeeper, you know. It's only for a few weeks, isn't it? Let me know in good time so that I can find somewhere for you, Meg.'

It seemed as good a time as any to talk about her future. Meg said quietly, 'Doreen, I'd like to go on housekeeping; if Mrs Culver will give me a reference I could get a job in some country house—and take Betsy with me—I'd probably get a cottage or a flat, and I'd much rather do that than live in London . . .'

Doreen looked at her with kindly tolerance. 'Don't be daft, love. Just you leave everything to Cora and me—we really know what's best for you. You've lived here too long; it's time you went into the world and had a look around.'

'I don't think it's my sort of world,' protested Meg doggedly. 'I like the country and keeping house and looking after people . . .'

'Nonsense,' said Doreen firmly. 'How can you be certain of that before you've lived somewhere else?' She added coaxingly, 'Cora and I do want you to be happy, darling; I know there wasn't much we could do about it while Mother was alive, but now we intend to see that you have some fun.'

There had been a lot they could have done, but Meg didn't say so; she loved her two pretty sisters and she wasn't a girl to bear a grudge.

All she said was, mildly, 'Well, Betsy and I will be here for two months—plenty of time to make plans.'

Doreen nodded her pretty head; she was looking thoughtful again. 'I don't suppose Mrs Culver will mind if I pop down to see you now and again?' And at Meg's look of surprise, 'Just to make sure that everything is OK ...' She gave herself away completely by adding, 'I wonder where he lives and what he does? I might be able to find out ...'

'Did you like him?' asked Meg.

'My dear Meg—grow up, do! He's got everything: looks—my goodness, he's got those all right—obviously a good job—probably chairman of something or other—and money. He's every girl's dream, ducky.'

'Oh, is he? I don't much care for him. Besides, he may be married.'

'But it's worth finding out. I must be off. I'll let you know when to expect the carrier to collect my furniture.' Doreen dropped a kiss on Meg's cheek. 'Be seeing you, darling. Has Cora phoned?'

'Last week. I expect she's busy; the boys have half term.

Getting into the car, Doreen said, 'I'm broke—this cashmere dress, but it's worth every penny. You must get yourself some decent clothes, love. You look—well—dowdy!'

She sped away with a wave and Meg stood in the porch, shivering a little in the cold wind, aware that her sister was quite right. A housekeeper should be decently but soberly dressed, and she would need a couple of overalls.

She would go into Hertford in the morning; she had a little money she had been hanging on to for emergencies, and since she was to be paid, she could safely spend it.

It took her some time to find what she wanted. Sober dresses suitable for a housekeeper seemed to be made for very large, tall women and she was size ten. She found something at last: dark grey with white collars and a little black bow; it did nothing for her whatsoever, but then it wasn't supposed to. She bought overalls too, blue and white checks with a white collar and neat belts, and since she had a little money over she bought Betsy two new aprons, old-fashioned with bibs which crossed over at the back and fastened with giant safety pins. Nothing would convince Betsy that nylon overalls saved time and labour; she had never fancied them, and she wasn't prepared to change her ideas at her time of life.

Another week went by. The solicitors, at last satisfied that all the parties concerned were not up to something unlawful, cautiously exchanged contracts and then, doubtless egged on by Mrs Culver, allowed them to be signed. The house was Mrs Culver's. All three of them had had to sign; Doreen had fetched Meg and had driven into Hertford, annoyed at what she called the waste of her precious time, but excited too, and Cora had driven herself from Kent, excited in a controlled way, anxious to get the business over and get back to her modern, split-level house with its well-kept garden and the double garage.

The whole business took only a very few minutes; they stood on the pavement outside the solicitor's office and looked at each other. 'I'd better come back to the house and get the pictures and silver,' said Cora. 'You heard what Mr Dutton said, Meg? The money will be paid into my account and I'll send you a cheque for your share, and Doreen, of course.' She looked at her younger sister. 'I expect you want to get back to the hospital. I'll take Meg back, collect my things and go home—I've a bridge party this afternoon.'

She tucked her arm into Meg's. 'Lovely to have it all settled. What a difference it's going to make.'

Meg said nothing at all. Doreen and Cora might be over the moon but she had just lost her home. She would rather have gone on living there until it fell in ruins about her ears; what use was the money to her if she had to use it to buy some ghastly basement flat? She swallowed back tears and got into Cora's car.

A week later Mrs Culver moved in. There had been a small van load of furniture first with instructions as to where it was to be put and at ten o'clock in the morning the Rolls-Royce had come to a quiet halt in front of the door and the new owner had stepped out, helped, Meg was annoyed to see, by her son, massive and calm and for some reason faintly amused. That the amusement had been engendered by her own sober appearance never entered her head. She welcomed Mrs Culver with shy dignity, and led the way to the drawing-room.

'I expect you'd like coffee. I'll bring it.' She glanced at Mr Culver. 'You'll have a cup, Mr Culver?'

'Thank you, yes.' He glanced round the room. 'I see you've had the time to arrange my mother's things.'

And when she said yes, he asked, 'The valuer has been?'

'Yes. He'll write to Mrs Culver.'

That lady was sitting back comfortably, taking no part in the conversation. Meg suspected that she was in the habit of leaving business matters to her son. She got herself out of the room and hurried to the kitchen to get the coffee tray.

'They're 'ere,' said Betsy, unnecessarily. ''E's 'ere too. A proper gent.'

Meg had her own ideas about that, but there was no time to discuss the man. She whipped up the tray and went back with it, and set it down on the lamp table by Mrs Culver's chair.

'Where's your cup?' asked the older woman.

'My cup?' Meg echoed.

'Yes, dear. Go and fetch it. Ralph hasn't much time, and he wants to be sure that there are no loose ends.'

Meg fetched another cup and saucer and sat down on a little chair as far from Mr Culver as she dared without being rude. He gave her a hooded glance.

'I wish merely to thank you for the help you've given my mother. Without you, she would have been unable to settle in so quickly. We're grateful. Do we owe you anything? Are there any outstanding bills?'

Meg said that, no, there weren't. 'Willy will be up tomorrow morning on his way to school and will fill the coal scuttles, and he'll come again in the afternoon on his way back home. The gardener starts on Monday.'

Mr Culver finished his coffee and got up. 'I think you'll be happy here, Mother. You know where I am if you need me, my dear.' He crossed the room and kissed her cheek, and nodded austerely to Meg. 'I'll see myself out.'

Meg poured more coffee, and Mrs Culver said, 'Such a good son—never interferes, you know, but always there when I want him. So convenient. He's just like his father.'

Meg looked at her companion with something like respect. If his father had been like him, then she must have had her work cut out—but perhaps he had loved her very much and never let her see the cold mockery and impatience—or perhaps it was Meg herself who induced those. She thought that probably it was; she had had no

practice in turning a man up sweet. She murmured
suitably and asked what Mrs Culver would like for lunch.

It took only a few days to settle into a routine. Mrs
Culver liked her breakfast in bed, which meant that Meg
and Betsy could eat their own meal and get on with the
household chores. Even with Mrs Griffith's help there
was plenty of work to be got through, and they did the
bulk of it in the early mornings. Mrs Culver's own car
had arrived with her chauffeur and she was out a good
deal, which gave Meg time to see to the washing and
ironing and help Betsy with the meals, so that tasks such
as arranging the flowers and setting the table for meals
could be done when that lady was at home, tasks which
Meg concluded were quite suitable for a housekeeper.
She had no doubt that Mrs Culver had little idea of what
went on behind the scenes; she was charming, easy and
very kind, and had very likely grown up and lived all her
life with people to do her bidding.

But it had been a surprise to Meg when Mrs Culver
had insisted on her taking her meals with her. And when
she had demurred, she had insisted, 'Nonsense, child.
You've sat at this table all your life; you will continue to
do so or upset me very much.'

So Meg sat at the table she had laid so carefully, getting
up to clear the dishes and fetch the food from the kitchen,
for Betsy had enough to do and her legs hurt in any case,
and she entirely approved of the arrangement. The dear
soul still thought of her as the lady of the house. Mrs
Culver was a nice enough lady, indeed, one couldn't wish
for a better, but there had been Collinses living there for
a long time, and she didn't take easily to change.

Meg was happy; she was still in her own home, she
enjoyed the work even though her days were long and
there was little time to get into the garden. Cora had
phoned to say that her share of the money was paid into

her account and to ask, rather casually, if she were happy. And when she had a satisfactory answer, 'Then I'll not bother you, Meg; let me know when you leave and I'll help in any way I can.'

She had a much longer call from Doreen, who wasted little time on questions but plunged at once into her news. She had discovered who Mr Culver was—a Professor, a consultant radiologist, based at one of the big teaching hospitals but with a large area to cover. 'He's well known,' said Doreen, 'goes to any number of hospitals for consultations—one of the best men in his field— Europe too. When is he going to visit his mother, Meg?'

'I've no idea. Did you want to see him about something? Shall I ask Mrs Culver?'

'I wish you'd grow up, Meg! Of course I want to see him, but only to get to know him. He's not married . . .'

Meg tried to imagine him as a future brother-in-law. 'He's quite old,' she pointed out in her practical manner.

'Rubbish—thirty-eight at the most. Quite brilliant at his work, too—he'll end up with a knighthood.'

'I thought you were keen on that registrar . . .'

'Oh, him! Listen, darling, if you hear that he's coming down to see his mother, give me a ring, will you?'

'Why?' asked Meg, being deliberately dim. She heard her sister's exasperated sigh as she hung up.

As it happened she had no chance to do that, and she was glad, for it smacked of disloyalty to Mrs Culver and to him. After all, she was in Mrs Culver's employ. The Professor walked in as they sat at lunch a day or two later. He had a dirty, half-starved dog under one arm which was cringing away from the sight of them, and Meg got up at once and said, 'Oh, the poor beast, let me have him. Have you come to lunch? There's plenty . . .'

It was a quiche Lorraine and she had just begun to cut it.

'Take it back to keep warm, Meg,' said Mrs Culver, 'it won't spoil for ten minutes or so. Bring a towel or something with you to put that dog on.'

The Professor stood, the animal still in his arms, waiting for Meg to come back. 'Found him in the road— been knocked down and left. Not hurt, I fancy, and, by the look of him, lost or abandoned.'

His mother rose to the occasion. 'Just what we could do with here—a guard dog. What is he?'

'Difficult to say. Ah, there you are—if you will put the towel on that table I'll take a look at him. A little warm milk perhaps?'

Meg went off to the kitchen again and came back with a bowl of milk, standing patiently while he examined the beast with gentle hands. 'Nothing broken.' He glanced at her and smiled. 'Just worn out, hungry and frightened. He'll be a splendid addition to the household.'

Meg proffered the milk; it disappeared with the speed of dust into a vacuum cleaner. 'There's a big box and some old blankets. I'll fetch them.'

'A nice child,' observed Mrs Culver when she had gone, 'and so sensible.'

'And a good housekeeper, I hope?'

'Excellent. I've been to visit Kate; she's doing well, but it will be a month at least ...'

'No need to hurry her,' said the Professor easily, 'since Meg suits you so well. No problems?'

'None, my dear. And she is so happy to be here. It must be dreadful for her having to give up her home to strangers.'

'Do you see anything of her sisters?' He glanced at his mother. 'I met her younger sister—a very pretty girl; she's at the Royal—staff nurse hoping to be made a Sister. She had no regrets leaving here, nor, I understand, had her elder sister.'

'The married one—I believe she's just as handsome. Are you on your way home, dear, or are you going back to town?'

'Back to town. I've a dinner date. But may I have lunch?'

Meg came back with the box and blankets and the dog was laid gently down and promptly went to sleep. Which left her free to fetch the quiche back and lay another place. She put the plates before Mrs Culver and said in her calm way, 'If you wanted to talk together I'll go away . . .'

'No need,' said the Professor before his mother could speak. 'Besides, we have to plan this animal's future. I'll phone the vet if I may, Mother, and if he's not injured, presumably he may stay?'

'Of course, my dear.' Mrs Culver turned to Meg. 'You know about dogs, Meg?'

'Oh, yes, Mrs Culver.' Nothing in her quiet voice betrayed the fact that she would have to get up earlier than ever to take him for a walk, that he would have to be groomed, fed and generally looked after. Not that she minded; she liked animals, and he would be company for Silky.

'Then that settles the matter. If you're not already engaged, Mother, I'll come over after church on Sunday and take you back for lunch.'

So he can't live far away, thought Meg, collecting plates and piling them tidily on a tray and carrying it out to the kitchen, where she loaded it up again with light-as-air castle puddings and hot jam sauce.

'Your cook is excellent,' observed the Professor, accepting a second helping.

'Oh, but Meg made these, didn't you, dear?'

His look of polite astonishment annoyed Meg; he could have no opinion of her at all! She said, 'Yes, as a matter of fact, I did,' in a tart voice and went to fetch the coffee.

'Don't you like her, dear?' asked his mother.

The look on his face gave her food for thought. 'I hardly know her,' he said at length. 'I dare say she might grow on one—missed when she's no longer there . . .'

'Such a waste,' said Mrs Culver vaguely, watching him. 'And so easily overlooked, especially when her sisters are with her.'

As Meg came back in with the tray the Professor got up to close the door behind her and watched her pour the coffee. She was wearing the severe grey dress and she had pinned up her pale brown hair into a tidy bun, under the impression that it made her look like a housekeeper. She was really nothing to look at; he was at a loss to understand why the thought of her crossed his mind from time to time. She handed him his cup and looked at him with her lovely grey eyes. They were cool and clear, like a child's. She said, 'It was kind of you to rescue the dog. I'll take great care of him.'

'Yes, I know. That's why I brought him here.' He smiled, and his severe expression melted into a charm which took her by surprise. She didn't like him, but just for a moment she glimpsed another man entirely.

She slipped away presently, pleading some household duty which kept her occupied until she heard the Rolls sigh its way down the drive. By then she had helped Betsy with the washing up, rubbed up the silver and got the tea-tray ready. It was Betsy's hour or so of peace and quiet, and Mrs Culver would doubtless be dozing. Meg went to look at the dog and found him awake, cringing in his box. She fed him, bathed some of the dirt and dust from him, tended his pathetically cracked paws and went to let the vet in.

They knew each other vaguely; years ago when her

father had been alive there had been dogs and cats and ponies. He was a grouchy old man but a splendid vet. He examined the dog carefully, pronounced him half starved, in need of rest and bruised from his accident. 'But he'll live,' he said. 'God alone knows what breed he is, but he's a nice enough beast. You're looking after him?' He looked at her enquiringly. 'Professor Culver said that he would be here with you ... He would have taken him to his home but he's only there at the weekends; a London flat is no place for dogs.'

Meg longed to ask where the Professor lived, but she didn't. At least she had learned something; that he had a flat in London. She listened carefully to the vet's instructions, offered him tea, which he refused, and saw him out to his car. By the time she had settled the dog again it was tea time.

A busy day, she reflected, getting ready for bed at the end of the day. It struck her that she earned every penny of the money Mrs Culver paid her, for she had little time to call her own. She set her alarm clock half an hour earlier than usual because she would have to take the dog out and feed him before starting on the morning's chores, and she found herself wondering what the Professor was doing. Lolling in an easy chair in a comfortable sitting-room, waited on hand and foot, she decided. Despite his kindness over the dog, her opinion of him was low.

He arrived on Sunday, expressed satisfaction at the dog's appearance, refused refreshment and ushered his mother out to the car. He settled her in the front seat and then turned back to speak to Meg, who was standing sedately by the front door. 'What will you call him?' he asked.

'Well, nothing at the moment. I thought that Mrs Culver or you ...'

'We leave it to you.' He smiled his charming smile

once more. 'Enjoy your afternoon, Meg.'

Meg, indeed! she thought indignantly, though of course she was employed by his mother and he had every right to address her in such a fashion. Perhaps he thought it might keep her in her place. She went indoors and made up the fire in the sitting-room, gave the dog a meal, took him for a short run in the garden, and went along to the kitchen. She and Betsy had their afternoon planned; lunch on a tray for Meg and a peaceful hour or so for Betsy in her chair by the Aga. They would have an early tea too, and there might even be time to potter in the garden. It was a miserably grey day, but Meg never let the weather bother her.

The afternoon was all that she had hoped for; accompanied by the now devoted animal, she repaired to the potting shed and, tied in her sacking apron, pricked out seedlings and transplanted wallflowers. Then she went to her tea, sitting at the kitchen table with Betsy opposite her and Silky and the dog sitting in a guarded friendship on the rug before the Aga. Betsy had made a cake that morning; the mixture had been too much for the cake tin, she explained guilelessly, so that there was a plate of little cakes as well as hot buttered toast and Meg's strawberry jam and strong tea in the brown earthenware pot which Betsy favoured.

They cleared away together; Meg fed the animals and then got into her old duffle coat and took the dog for a gentle walk. 'You'll have to have a name,' she told him, suiting her pace to his still painful paws. 'How about Lucky? Because that's what you are, you know!'

Then she stopped to rub the rough fur on the top of his head, and he gave her a devoted look. He was beginning to look happy and he had stopped cringing. Back in the house, she settled him in the kitchen with a bone and went to tidy herself. It was time to be the housekeeper again.

The sitting-room looked charming as she went into it; she had made a good fire, there were flowers and pot plants scattered around the tables, and shaded lamps. She began to draw the curtains and saw the lights of the Rolls-Royce sweep up the drive, and she went into the hall and opened the door.

'Oh, how nice it all looks!' declared Mrs Culver. 'Meg, you have no idea how happy I am to be living here—to have found such a delightful home, and you with it, too!'

She slid off her fur coat and Meg took it from her, thinking that she had done just that so many times for her mother when she had been alive and well. She glanced up and found Professor Culver's dark eyes on her, his thoughtful look disturbing. She turned away and suggested coffee, and, 'There's a fire in the sitting-room,' she pointed out.

'No coffee, Meg—we'll have a drink. You'll stay a few minutes, Ralph?'

He had taken off his car coat and thrown it on to the oak settle against a wall. 'Yes, of course.' His eyes were still on Meg. He asked, 'Have you named the dog?'

Yes, I'd like to call him Lucky. It was lucky for him when you met him . . .'

'An appropriate name. I've never believed in luck, but I think that perhaps I have been mistaken about that. You've had a pleasant afternoon?'

She looked surprised. 'Yes, thank you.' She sought feverishly for an excuse to get away from his stare. 'I must take Lucky out . . . Unless you need me for anything, Mrs Culver?'

'No, my dear, off you go. Wrap up warmly; it's a chilly evening.'

Meg nipped off to the kitchen, thinking that sometimes her employer talked to her as though she were her daughter. She put on the duffle coat again and encountered Betsy's surprised look. 'You've just been out with the beast,' she pointed out, ''ad yer forgotten, Miss Meg?'

Meg opened the kitchen door and started off down the stone passage leading to the garden. Lucky, anxious to please, even if reluctant, trotted beside her.

'No—it's all right, Betsy, it's only until the Professor's gone.'

The remark puzzled Betsy; it puzzled Meg too. Just because one didn't like a person it didn't mean to say that one had to run away from them, and wasn't she being a bit silly, trudging round the garden on such a beastly evening just because Professor Culver was ill-mannered enough to stare so?

CHAPTER THREE

Two or three days passed. The weather was what was to be expected for the time of year: rain and a flurry of snow, and then a lovely day with a blue sky and an icy wind; Mrs Culver kept to the house for the first two days and then decided to accept a lunch invitation with friends in Ware. Meg phoned Noakes, the chauffeur, who now lived in the village with his wife, and watched her employer borne away before calling to Lucky and taking him for a brisk walk. It had certainly turned cold; she settled him with Silky before the kitchen fire, had bread and cheese and a great pot of tea with Betsy sitting at the kitchen table, and then went away to make up the fires and get the tea tray ready; Mrs Culver would probably be cold and tired when she got back, and a few scones might be a good idea. She returned to the kitchen and made a batch while Betsy sat by the Aga, having what she called a bit of a shut-eye.

Mrs Culver arrived back rather sooner than Meg had expected, and she didn't look very well.

'I'm cold,' she complained. 'I mean cold inside; I'd like a cup of tea . . .'

'It's quite ready, Mrs Culver,' said Meg soothingly, 'and there's a lovely fire in the drawing-room. I'll bring the tray in there.' She drew a chair to the fire. 'I made some scones—you'll enjoy those.'

Only Mrs Culver didn't; she drank several cups of tea, her nice face becoming more and more flushed, and when Meg suggested that she might like to go to her bed, she agreed without a fuss.

'Well, you stay there for a few minutes; I'll see to the

electric blanket and warm your nightie. I won't be long.'

She was barely ten minutes, and when she got back it was to find Mrs Culver shivering and reluctant to leave her chair. It took a good deal of coaxing to get her up the stairs and into her room, and once there Meg helped her undress and tucked her up in bed, and then proceeded to sponge off Mrs Culver's carefully applied make-up and comb her hair.

'I feel awful,' said Mrs Culver.

Meg refrained from telling her that she looked awful and worse every minute. 'A chill,' she said bracingly. 'I'm going to get you a warm drink and phone Doctor Woods. He'll give you something to make you feel better.'

She had known Doctor Woods all her life, and he had been in and out of the house for weeks before her mother died. She liked his forthright, gruff manner, and he for his part knew that she wasn't a girl to panic.

By the time he arrived, some twenty minutes later, Mrs Culver was looking decidedly worse.

"Flu,' said Doctor Woods. 'There's a lot of it about. Got anyone to fetch a prescription?'

'No. Willy has gone and there's only Betsy. I'll have to phone Noakes; he's the chauffeur and lives in the village. He'll have to come here and get the car . . .'

'Tell you what, I'll leave enough of these to last until tomorrow; let the chauffeur get the rest in the morning. I'll be in again tomorrow some time; you're sensible enough to let me know if you get worried.'

He closed his bag and started getting into his coat. 'Any family?'

'A son—Professor Culver . . .'

'You don't say? Brilliant man in his field. You'd better let him know. No danger as far as I can see, but all the same . . .'

'I'll go and do it right away,' promised Meg.

'You look a bit peaked yourself, Meg. Working too

hard, are you? You could do with a holiday. Where are those sisters of yours?'

'Well, Cora has her own home and family, as you know, and Doreen's at the hospital still.'

He grunted, which could have meant anything, patted her on the shoulder and went out to his car, muttering.

Mrs Culver was dozing; she looked ill, but no worse. Meg went downstairs and went to the study and picked up the telephone. The Professor's number was written neatly on a card beside it, and she dialled it. A London number—and a rather severe voice told her that it was Professor Culver's residence. 'Is the Professor there?' Meg asked. 'And if he is, will you tell him it's his mother's housekeeper?'

'Be good enough to wait,' said the voice, and she glanced at the clock. It was getting on for seven o'clock; he might be changing for the evening, in the shower, tossing down a sherry with some blonde beauty before going out to dine . . .

'Yes?' said the Professor's voice in her ear. Very calm and unhurried.

Terse, thought Meg. Well, two could be that. 'Mrs Culver came back from a visit this afternoon not feeling well. I've put her to bed and Doctor Woods has been to see her. He says she has 'flu. He thought that you should be told. She's on an antibiotic, and at present she's dozing.'

His voice was still calm and unhurried. 'I'll be with you within the hour. Give me Doctor Woods' telephone number, will you?'

Unfeeling monster, thought Meg, and gave it before hanging up with a speed which gave him no chance to say anything else.

She went to have another look at Mrs Culver, who was still asleep, and then went to the kitchen to tell Betsy. 'So there'll be no need to have dinner in the dining-room,' she concluded, 'we'll have it here when Professor Culver has gone.'

'Such a nice fish soufflé we've planned, too. I've got it all ready to cook.'

'Well, we'll still have it later on. The soup won't spoil, will it, and I made that upside-down pudding—is it already in the oven?'

'Yes, Miss Meg, but it'll come to no 'arm.'

'I'll make a jug of lemonade for Mrs Culver and beat up an egg in milk and put a pinch of nutmeg with it . . .' Her eye lighted on Lucky, watching her from his bed by the Aga. 'I'd better take Lucky out now.'

Lucky had no taste for a cold evening; perhaps he had had too many of them. Ten minutes was enough for him, and Meg saw to his and Silky's suppers and made the lemonade, adding ice and taking it upstairs.

Mrs Culver was awake and inclined to be peevish, but she allowed Meg to turn her pillows and sit her up with a gossamer wool shawl around her, and she obediently drank her lemonade. 'And presently I'll bring you egg and milk. I make it rather nicely; Mother loved it . . . Here's the bell, Mrs Culver; ring if you want me. I'll be in the kitchen, but I'll leave the doors open so that I'll be able to hear.'

Mrs Culver nodded and murmured and closed her eyes again; she really looked poorly and it would be a little while before the antibiotics did their work. Meg sped downstairs again, rearranging the running of the house to fit in with nursing the invalid. No difficult task for her, for she had had experience enough with her mother. She was crossing the hall when she saw the lights of a car coming up the drive. Professor Culver had made good time. She opened the door and he got out and gave her a civil good evening.

He threw off his coat, took her arm and walked her into the sitting-room. 'I've telephoned Doctor Woods.

Before I see my mother I should like to know what you think, Meg.' He added brusquely, 'You've had experience of elderly ladies. Are you worried?'

She said coldly, 'Don't imagine, Professor, that because I nursed my mother for several months I'm an expert on such matters. My mother died of congestive heart failure; as far as I can remember, she never had 'flu.'

She was quite unprepared for his contrition. He turned her round to face him, still holding her arm. 'I'm sorry—that was unpardonable of me. I think what I meant to say was that you must have an understanding of elderly ladies and can perhaps set my mind at rest. My mother is a volatile little lady; I'm never quite sure ...'

She said at once, 'I don't think you have need to worry, Professor. Mrs Culver is in good hands, I assure you. Doctor Woods is a splendid man; he's coming again in the morning. I'll take good care of her, but if you would like to have a nurse for her ...'

'The idea hadn't entered my head. You're a most capable young woman, and very sensible. I'm going up to see her now.'

He left her standing there, fuming. To be taken so for granted; she was to run the house as usual, presumably, as well as look after his mother, and, unless she was very much mistaken, she wouldn't get much sleep for the next night or two. She went along to the kitchen, her colour so high that Betsy wanted to know if she had the 'flu as well.

She was beating egg and milk when the Professor came in. He stood for a moment, watching her. 'That's for my mother. Good. Something smells delicious.'

And when Betsy looked round he smiled with such charm at her that she said, 'Leek soup—me own make, an' fish soufflé an' as nice an upside-down pudding as ever Miss Meg made. Dab 'and at it, she is.'

'May I stay to supper?'

Meg didn't trust that humble voice one little bit, but before she could say anything, Betsy observed, 'Plenty for three!'

Meg went to the door with the egg and milk. 'I'll stay for a while with Mrs Culver . . .'

The little tray was whisked from her. 'No, I'll see that she drinks this while you dish up.'

He was gone before she could frame an answer.

He was back in ten minutes. 'She's dozed off again; she drank it all—it looked revolting.' He smiled suddenly at Meg. 'Would you like me to stay overnight?'

She ladled soup. 'Heavens, no. If you're quite happy about your mother there's no need for you to stay. I guarantee I can get Doctor Woods if I'm worried.'

'I'm a doctor too,' he pointed out.

'Oh, are you? Doreen said you were a radiologist.' She blushed, because it must seem to him that they had been discussing him.

He watched the blush with interest. 'I am, but I was a doctor first, if you see what I mean.'

He sat down at the table and Lucky went to sit beside him, resting his woolly head on his knee. The Professor stroked it gently. 'Have you found a flat yet?' he asked idly.

Meg gave him an exasperated look. 'I haven't been up to London to look for one.'

'From choice, or has my mother overlooked the fact that you should have a day to yourself each week?'

'The question hasn't arisen,' she told him coldly. 'I'm very happy as matters stand.'

His eyes narrowed. 'But you do realise that once Kate returns you are to leave?'

They were sitting opposite to each other at the scrubbed table with Betsy at its head, half-way through their soup.

'Naturally I know that. Mrs Culver told me that Kate

will be coming here in three weeks or so. I'm sure that Doreen will find me something—somewhere to live until I can buy a flat.'

'They're not very thick on the ground in London, nor are they cheap. What are you going to do?'

Meg collected up the soup plates. 'I can't see that that is any concern of yours, Professor Culver,' she said frostily.

'Which means that you have no idea.' He accepted the fish soufflé from Betsy, and when they had eaten it, collected the plates and took them over to the sink.

'Now there 'ain't no call fer yer to do that,' cried Betsy. 'Just you sit down while I dish that pudding, sir.' She trotted over to the Aga, tutting indignantly and secretly delighted with his help. She gave him the lion's share of the pudding, and when they had eaten it offered a cup of tea.

He accepted with alacrity, complimented them on the delicious meal, sat back comfortably in his chair and, to Meg's utter surprise, when they had drunk it, declared his intention of washing up.

'You won't know 'ow, sir!' said Betsy.

'Then you can sit there by the stove and instruct me while Meg does whatever needs doing for my mother.'

Meg wished most fervently that she was a statuesque beauty, so that she could have swept out of the kitchen with style. Instead she took her small person out of the room with something of a flounce, unaware of the amusement in the Professor's eyes.

'The nerve!' she muttered, going upstairs. 'Coming here and eating our supper and telling me what to do! He's insufferable!'

But the face which she presented to Mrs Culver was kind and smiling. She spent some time making her comfortable, took her temperature, sponged her face and hands, gave her a drink, assured her that she was getting better already and straightened the bed.

Surely the Professor would be gone by now, she thought as she went downstairs, but he wasn't. He was at the sink, making heavy weather of the cleaning of the saucepans and enjoying a chat with Betsy.

'If you want to see Mrs Culver ...' Meg began severely.

'I must go now,' he finished with a meekness she didn't believe. He wiped out the last saucepan, washing his hands and then putting on his jacket. When he had left the kitchen Betsy said comfortably, 'Now there's a nice gent for yer, Miss Meg. Never washed dishes in his life before, I dare swear, and did them well enough too.'

'Any fool can wash up,' said Meg loftily. 'I hope he goes soon; we've got to plan ...' She stopped, because Betsy was looking uncomfortable.

The Professor was standing just behind her, his hands in his pockets, listening with interest.

'Mother is asleep already. I'm going now.' He spoke pleasantly. 'If it doesn't disturb your plans, I should like to visit her tomorrow morning.'

He bade Betsy an affable goodnight and walked out of the kitchen, and Meg went after him. In the hall she said, 'I'm sorry I was rude, Professor Culver. You must come whenever you want.'

'Of course. Be good enough to ring me if you're worried—and thank you for my supper. Not quite the evening I had intended, but none the less a good deal more interesting. And I leave my mother in good hands.'

He stood towering over her, staring down at her upturned face. Probably a very nice man, she thought illogically, if one happened to like him. The last thing she expected was his sudden swoop and his kiss on her cheek. 'Thank you, little Meg,' he said softly, and let himself out of the house.

An action which left her with a head full of mixed emotions.

Mrs Culver, already feverish, became more so as the evening wore on, and Meg saw that it would make more sense if she were to get ready for bed and then curl up on one of the easy chairs in Mrs Culver's room. At least she was able to doze off each time her patient did; all the same, she was glad enough when morning came and Mrs Culver, refreshed with a cool drink, her bed smoothed and her pillows turned, dropped off into real sleep at last. Too late for Meg to go to her own bed; she had a shower and dressed, yawning her head off as she did so, and then went down to join Betsy in a cup of tea before putting on the duffle coat and taking Lucky for his walk. Mrs Culver was still sleeping peacefully when she got back, so she obediently ate the breakfast Betsy had ready and then, leaving the dear soul to clear the kitchen and start preparations for the day's meals, went along to set the fires going.

There was no point in lighting the drawing-room fire, but there had better be one in the sitting-room, she thought. She was arranging coals on the wood and paper when Professor Culver came quietly into the room to startle her with his 'Good morning, Meg.'

She was kneeling before the grate, and turned an unmade-up face to him. It was a tired, pale face too, framed by a rather untidy head of hair, and there was a smear of coal dust on one cheek. 'My goodness, don't you get up early?' she exclaimed.

He said softly, 'At least I went to bed. From the look of you, you didn't. How is my mother?'

'Sleeping. She had a restless night, just dozing now and then, but she dropped off soundly after I'd tidied her up and she's had a drink. She's still asleep.' She got to her feet. 'You'd like to go up . . .?'

He didn't answer her, but got his lighter from a pocket

and bent down to light the fire. When he was sure that it was well and truly alight, he said, 'Yes, I should.' To her surprise he added, 'Will you be able to catch up on your sleep during the day?'

Meg lied briskly, 'Oh, yes, thank you,' and watched him go up the stairs before telephoning to Noakes, who arrived with commendable swiftness to take the prescription for Mrs Culver's pills and who accepted the shopping list Meg had made out without demur. 'Can you manage, Miss?' he asked kindly. 'Anything I can do to help out?'

He was a kindly man as well as being an excellent chauffeur. 'Well, no, thank you, Noakes,' said Meg. 'Mrs Griffiths comes today, so we can manage very well, but I dare say I might have to ask you to do some more shopping until Mrs Culver is well again.'

She took him along to the kitchen and Betsy made him a cup of tea while Meg went back to the sitting-room to see how the fire was doing. She found the Professor there, putting on coals.

'Mother is decidedly better,' he informed her. 'She'll have to stay in bed for a few days, though. Can you manage? Do you need help of any sort?'

She was surprised for the second time. 'Mrs Griffiths is coming today—she comes three times a week to do the rough,' and at his puzzled look, 'floors and scrubbing and windows,' she explained. 'Betsy and I can manage the rest easily enough.'

He eyed her small person thoughtfully. 'You're rather small,' he observed. 'Quality not quantity, no doubt. Couldn't one of your sisters come over to help out for a day or so?'

She turned a look of amazement on him. 'They couldn't spare the time; besides, I think you're making a fuss about nothing, Professor Culver; I ran this house and nursed my mother for almost a year . . .'

'I stand corrected.' He was laughing at her, and she felt annoyed.

When he added that he would have to go, she offered him coffee in such a stiff voice that he refused at once. 'Will you ask Doctor Woods to give me a ring? He knows my number. I'll telephone you this evening. In the meantime, if you're worried, don't hesitate to ring my home—you have the number. Good morning, Meg—I'll see myself out.'

The day was filled with small, tiresome tasks which had to be done as well as a visit from Doctor Woods, who pronounced himself satisfied with his patient's progress, advised two or three days in bed and a light diet, gave instructions about pills and promised to call the following day.

'And you look as though you could do with a good sleep,' he informed Meg. 'See that you get one.'

Meg said that she would, knowing that it wasn't very likely; Mrs Culver, charming though she was in good health, was a bad patient.

The day drew to a close with a call from Professor Culver, full of searching questions. He thanked her austerely, told her that he would be along in the morning, and rang off. Meg, peevish after a day that had held no quiet moment for her, removed the frown from her face and eventually went to tell Mrs Culver that her son would visit her the following morning and to persuade her to take just a little of the dainty supper she had prepared.

But at least Mrs Culver slept for most of the night. Meg, after several hours' sleep, was quite her usual calm self by the time Professor Culver arrived. He took a good look at her as he came through the door.

'That's better,' he observed. 'I take it my mother had a good night and so did you?'

He was in no hurry to go; he accepted Meg's polite offer of coffee and said that since he was there he might as well stay and see Doctor Woods. Meg offered him the daily papers and excused herself on the grounds of jobs to do around the house. There was a nice fire burning, and he looked comfortable enough sitting beside it—thoroughly at home, in fact. But of course, she reminded herself, it was his home, or at least his mother's.

Doctor Woods came early just as Meg had made her patient comfortable for the morning. Mrs Culver was sitting up against her pillows, nicely wrapped in a pretty bed jacket, her hair tied back with a ribbon, still pale but decidedly better.

'No need to come for a couple of days,' said Doctor Woods, 'unless you want me, Meg. An hour or two out of bed tomorrow and then try going downstairs on the following day. I'll see you then.'

He bustled downstairs again, and Meg took in a fresh tray of coffee, heaving a sigh of relief when the two men left together, the Professor in his gleaming Rolls, Doctor Woods in his elderly Rover.

Professor Culver had paused at the door to tell her that he had to go to Edinburgh that afternoon and would telephone from there. 'I shall be away for three days,' he told her austerely. His goodbye was equally austere.

'And as far as I'm concerned,' declared Meg to Lucky, who was standing beside her as she watched him drive away, 'he may go for three years. It'll be nice to get back to normal again.'

It may have been nice, but she had to confess that it was unexpectedly dull; the Professor, tiresome though he was, had supplied an interest in her days. He had left her feeling unsettled, and it was a relief when Doctor Woods pronounced Mrs Culver well enough to resume normal life as long as she took care not to go out until the cold, wet spell was over. Which meant that Meg spent a good deal of time playing cribbage and two-handed patience with her while still contriving to do her usual household chores. Of the Professor there was no sign, although he telephoned his mother each day.

The wet February weather suddenly became a premature spring; it wouldn't last, but Mrs Culver took advantage of the mild, sunny days to visit friends in London and, since she felt no ill effects from that, another visit to see how Kate was getting on. She came back from that in the best of spirits, to tell Meg that her housekeeper would be able to return in two weeks' time.

'She won't be able to do a great deal, of course, but if Betsy would stay . . . do you suppose she would, Meg? And if you could persuade Mrs Griffiths to come for an extra day?' She smiled kindly at Meg. 'So now you'll be able to go to London and live nearer your sister. Has she found a flat for you yet?'

Somehow Meg had allowed her future to become vague; anything could happen, she had told herself, and the weeks had slipped by almost unnoticed. Doreen had phoned once or twice, but she had been more concerned with her new flat and whether or not Meg had seen any more of Professor Culver than with Meg's future. She had been living in cloud cuckoo land, and the sooner she returned to more realistic plans for the future the better.

She answered her companion in her usual calm manner. 'That's good news, Mrs Culver; shall I ask Betsy to come and see you tomorrow morning? I'm sure she'll be very glad to stay here. I'll ask Mrs Griffiths . . .'

She phoned Doreen that evening and was barely given time to tell her news. 'Couldn't be better, Meg—there's a basement flat for sale in a quite decent side street off Stamford Street—that's just behind Waterloo Station— very handy if you get a job in the City. I'll go to the agent's in the morning and I'll ring up tomorrow . . .' she hung up.

Meg sat down quietly to think. It was all very well for Doreen to find her somewhere to live; she had no job and no idea what to do, anyway. It would be far better for her to find something out of London; it would have to be domestic, for that was all she could do. She took herself off to bed, feeling worried.

Doreen phoned again the next day. Meg was to get a day off; the flat was just what she needed. It wouldn't need much done to it, and her share of the money from the house would be enough to pay for it and leave a little nest egg over.

'But I'll need to get a job,' said Meg, and was swamped by Doreen's brisk, 'Of course you will, but let's get this flat settled first. Let me know which day you're coming and I'll meet you.'

Mrs Culver thought it a splendid idea. 'You have a day in town, dear,' she said. 'I'm quite well again, and Betsy can look after me. Noakes shall drive you up and fetch you when you're ready; just let him know when and where.'

So Meg made her plans; she rang Doreen again and got the address of the flat, arranged with Noakes to take her there and fetch her again in the afternoon, and combed her rather scanty wardrobe for something to wear. Her jersey shirtwaister—by no means new, but it went well with her brown tweed coat. She had her wages in her purse and she would have liked to have done some shopping, but the flat wasn't anywhere near the shopping streets.

At the last minute Doreen telephoned to tell her to meet her at the hospital at midday. 'Wait in the entrance hall, love; I'll be off duty until four o'clock. We'll have a snack somewhere and then inspect the flat. The agent will meet us there and come back for the keys later.'

Meg had to wait for Doreen at the hospital; Noakes had deposited her at the entrance exactly at midday, promised to go to the flat at four to pick her up again, and had driven off. Meg whiled away the time wandering

round the entrance hall, a vast, forbidding place, its walls
hung with portraits of dead and gone medical men and
with absolutely nowhere to sit.

Doreen was wearing the cashmere dress again, with a
short suede jacket over it. She looked stunning, and there
was a young man with her who eyed Meg in some
astonishment. When introduced as Doctor Willis, he
said, 'I say, are you really Doreen's sister? You're not a
bit alike,' he added hastily.

It seemed that he was going to drive them to the flat.
He had half an hour to spare and nothing better to do,
and it wasn't very far.

All the streets looked alike to Meg, and when he turned
off Stamford Street into a narrow side street lined with
shabby houses, each with area steps leading to the
basements, she glanced around her with something like
horror. There wasn't a tree in sight, and not so much as a
laurel bush growing.

Doctor Willis drew up with a flourish with a cheerful,
'Here you are—out you get, girls. See you, Doreen.' He
nodded to Meg and drove off, and Doreen opened the
iron gate of the area behind them and led the way down
the steps.

The area was small, damp and cluttered with a variety
of bottles, and the door needed a coat of paint urgently. It
was opened as they reached it and the clerk from the
estate agents ushered them inside. He opened the inner
door at the same time; if he hadn't there wouldn't have
been room for the three of them in the lobby.

'Not kept you waiting?' asked Doreen breezily. The
man said no, certainly not; the half hour he had had to
stand around would be worth it if he could pull off the
sale. 'Quite a few people after this place,' he observed
heartily. 'I'll take you round and then leave you and
collect the key some time around four o'clock.'

The living-room was on the dark side, since the only

window looked out on to the area. It had a small fireplace, what the clerk erroneously described as fitted bookshelves on either side and which were in fact planks put up by some DIY enthusiast, and a pipe running up one wall which he dismissed with a wave of the hand. A door at the side led to a tiny kitchen with no window, which led in turn to the bedroom overlooking a forlorn garden with a row of dustbins along one wall and a tangle of grass. The bathroom had been built on at some time; the bath was stained by a continuously dripping tap and the washbasin was cracked; Meg didn't dare look at the toilet. The man said brightly, 'The fixtures are included in the price, of course,' and waved a hand at a small wall cupboard. Meg, feeling that she should show some interest, opened it. Inside there was a used tube of toothpaste, a piece of very old soap and a half-filled bottle of brilliantine. She closed the door again without saying anything and watched a very large spider disappear down the waste pipe of the bath. It was a depressing little room, and the previous owner—a man, decided Meg because of the brilliantine—had obviously thought the same, for one wall had been painted shrimp pink. He had either run out of paint or lost heart, for the other walls were white . . .

'Well, I'll leave you ladies to inspect the flat thoroughly——' the man gave them a bright smile, '—— redecorated and furnished, this place could be a little gem.'

They watched him go and went back to the living-room. It surprised Meg when Doreen said, 'He's right, you know. And you'll have enough money to have the place painted and papered.'

'Doreen, I don't think I could live here—not after home . . . there'd never by any sun, and it smells damp.'

Doreen took her arm. 'Look, love, you'll have a dear little home of your own and you're sure to get a job pretty soon. We're going down the road for something to eat—I saw a café in that row of shops on the corner—and then we'll come back and go over the place yard by yard.'

The café was small, with plastic tables and vinegar and tomato sauce arranged on each one. They had egg and chips and coffee, and Doreen pointed out that the shops on either side would provide day-to-day necessities without Meg having to walk miles.

They went back presently and went round the flat slowly. Meg tried hard to imagine living there and she couldn't. 'It's no good, Doreen,' she declared. 'I couldn't be happy here. I'm awfully grateful to you for finding it, but it's a kind of prison, isn't it? Is your flat like this?'

Doreen dealt with her with her usual briskness. 'No, love—it's in a modern block and of course it's . . .' She paused. 'You see, I've got a good job and I could afford to pay more—besides I got a mortgage. You must come and see it some time.' She frowned. 'What happens when you leave Mrs Culver, though—you'll have nowhere to go? I suppose Cora would have you for a little while, but you would have no hope of getting a job if you stayed there. It's much more sensible for you to snap this little place up and settle in—there'll be enough money for you to look round for a bit.' She glanced at her watch. 'I must go; I'm on duty in half an hour. I'll go to the corner and get a cab.' She kissed Meg. 'The clerk will be back for the key—when is Noakes coming for you?'

'About four o'clock.'

'Oh, good. Cheer up, love; Cora and I are quite sure that this is the best thing for you to do.' She gave Meg an affectionate pat on the shoulder and hurried away. Watching her go, Meg reflected that she really knew nothing of her two sisters' lives; they had lived away from home for several years now and they didn't regret leaving the pleasant old house and the peace and quiet of the country.

She fetched an empty tea chest from the kitchen, upended it and sat down. She would have liked a cup of tea, but the man from the estate agent's would be calling shortly for the key, and after that she wouldn't dare go to the café in case she missed Noakes. She would have to wait in the area, she supposed, and so she got up and went on another tour of inspection. It left her more convinced than ever that she couldn't possibly live there. When she got back she would look for a job as a housekeeper, au pair—anything rather than live in London.

The sky had clouded over, and it would be dark earlier than usual. The electricity had been cut off, naturally, and although she found the dark of the country quite unfrightening, she winced away from the idea of sitting there in the dusk. It was still barely four o'clock, she told herself; the key would be fetched very soon and she could wait outside for Noakes. In the meantime she thought about her future: Betsy was safe, which was a blessing; and Meg herself had quite a sum of money now that she had her share of the house sale. A cottage in some small town or village would cost far less than even the pokiest of flats in London, and she could surely find a job— anything that would bring in enough to feed and clothe her! She become so engrossed in her planning that she failed to hear a car draw up and a measured tread on the area steps. The thump of the door knocker brought her to her feet. It would be the man from the estate agent's. She went to the door and opened it, and Professor Culver strode past her to come to a halt in the living-room. 'Good God!' he said, and then, 'You aren't going to live here?'

The very sight of him, large and assured and unexpected, acted upon Meg in a surprising manner. She burst into tears.

The Professor didn't say a word, merely scooped her

against his massive shoulder and waited patiently while she sniffed and snorted and hiccupped.

When she finally heaved the last sobs, he offered a handkerchief and asked in a matter-of-fact voice, 'As bad as that, is it?'

'They want me to live here, but I can't—it's awful; there's a spider in the bath and there's no sun and all you can see out of the window are people's feet. They say I can have it done up and get a job, but I can't do any of the things people do in London—type and sell things, only they won't listen . . .'

'They?'

'Doreen and Cora. I know they think it's the best thing for me and I've always done what they suggested— they're clever, you see, but I really can't . . .'

He flung an arm round her shoulder. 'Let's look round?' he suggested.

When they were back in the living-room he said, 'I see what you mean—that's a frightful pink wall in the bathroom, and there's wood rot.'

'Oh, is that the smell in the kitchen?'

'Yes.' He left her to answer the knock on the door and came back with the clerk. 'Ready to go?' he asked her, and handed the man the key. 'The lady won't be buying this flat,' he observed pleasantly. 'Good day to you.'

He took Meg's arm and went ahead up the area steps on to the pavement. The Rolls was parked there, and the Professor opened the door and stowed her inside then got in beside her. Events had moved rather fast; Meg asked, 'Noakes is coming—how did you know where I was?'

'He told me. It seemed foolish for him to come back to town when I would be leaving at the same time.'

He drove off and turned into Stamford Street, and she thought about it before she said, 'Please don't tell Mrs Culver. She's so kind; I'll tell her that I have other plans, that I've got a job outside London.'

'Where?'

She said sharply, 'How should I know that until I've found something? But I'm good at housework and looking after people and shopping—there's bound to be something ...' They stopped at traffic lights and she added, 'I'm sorry I made such a fuss just now. Only I didn't expect you, and somehow you made the flat look so dreadful ... I can't explain.' She put a gloved hand up to her face. 'I must look awful.'

'You look like anyone else who's just had a good howl. Have you finished crying?'

She felt suddenly cross. 'Yes. If you hadn't been there I wouldn't have cried; I practically never do.'

'Good. Now that you're in a sensible frame of mind you will listen to what I have to say; and don't interrupt. I don't like to be interrupted.'

Meg glanced sideways at his profile. He looked stern and she could hardly blame him; she had made a fine fool of herself. She folded her hands on her lap and looked at them. She wouldn't say a word, whatever it was he was going to say to her.

CHAPTER FOUR

THE Professor slid the Rolls smoothly past an articulated lorry, making his way towards the A10.

'You have to find a home and a job,' he said austerely. 'I can offer you both.' If he heard Meg's surprised gasp he took no notice of it. 'You probably know that I'm a radiologist. Most of my work is done at Maud's, but I have a private practice just off Wigmore Street and I travel a good deal to other hospitals. I live here in London during the week; I have a small house here, but my home is at Much Hadham; I go there whenever possible and at the weekends. I have a secretary at my rooms and a receptionist to answer the phone, make appointments and so forth—not an arduous job, but it does, however, require someone with a pleasant voice and manner, who is a hard worker and willing to undertake errands and make the tea. There's a caretaker living in the basement and a small flatlet on the top floor which goes with the job. And since your heart is set on the country, there's no reason why you shouldn't spend the weekends there. There's an empty gardener's cottage in the grounds; until I can find a suitable man to live there and work for me you're welcome to go there whenever you want—there's plenty of gardening for you if you feel inclined.'

It seemed that he had no more to say. There was a lot of traffic—they were on the A10 by now, on the outskirts of the sprawling city. After a silence which Meg felt had lasted long enough, she asked, 'What's happened to the receptionist?'

He laughed. 'Any other girl would have asked how much money she was being offered and what the hours would be! She's leaving to get married.'

'Why me? I might not do! I can't type or do shorthand; I've never been inside an office.' A sudden thought struck her. 'You haven't offered me a job because I was silly just now?' She was being foolish—she was just beginning to realise what a marvellous job it would be. Wigmore Street was a far cry from the side street behind Waterloo Station. And there would be weekends to look forward to, but if all these delights were being offered out of pity she would have to refuse.

Her doubts were put at rest in no uncertain manner. 'Now you are being silly,' said the Professor. 'You're right for the job—a hard worker, a pleasant voice, patience—and by heavens, you'll need that sometimes— no young men to distract you, a real need to earn your own living and make a home for yourself. And I need someone to air the cottage until it's required for a gardener. A very convenient arrangement for us both.' He told her the salary. 'And that's the basic, of course; you'll get an increase every year. The hours are irregular at times—that's why the flat is rent free. The phone will be switched through each evening so that you can take messages. If you want to go out—but I don't imagine you will—the caretaker will take over.'

So she wouldn't want to go out! The nerve, thought Meg peevishly; how is he to know that I shan't meet someone—a young man who'll fall in love with me and sweep me off my feet? She spent half a minute pursuing this pleasant daydream and was brought down to earth by his, 'Well, will you consider it? Yes or no?'

Meg heard herself say yes, although she wasn't sure that she had meant to.

They were off the A10 now, on a secondary road going to Much Hadham, and Meg suddenly realised the fact. 'But I'm going to Hertingfordbury!' she exclaimed.

'I'll take you there shortly. You'd better see the

cottage. I'll give you a lift at weekends. Of course, you may not like it.'

But she did. They went through the village, past the Elizabethan cottages and the rather grand gentlemen's houses, past the Bishop's Palace, until he slowed the car and turned into an open gateway with a very small plaster and timber cottage tucked beside it.

If Meg had had any doubts about accepting the Professor's offer, they disappeared now. The cottage stood in a small garden, protected by iron railings, and it had an important porch which dwarfed the rest of the lodge. Even now, in the dusk of a late February evening, it looked enchanting. Meg couldn't get out fast enough to have a closer look at it.

Professor Culver produced a key, opened the stout door and switched on a light. The door opened on to the living-room, sparsely furnished although the table and chairs and dresser were old and well cared for. The fireplace was large, almost an inglenook, and the walls were white plaster. There was a small kitchen with a boiler for hot water, a bathroom in a pleasing shade of cream and a quite large bedroom, nicely furnished with a brass bedstead and an applewood dressing table and wardrobe.

Meg revolved slowly, taking it all in. 'And I can come here each weekend?' She wanted to make sure of that. 'That is, until you find a gardener. I can't believe it's true!'

He was standing leaning against a wall, watching her. 'I doubt if I'll find a man before the spring,' he said carelessly. 'Get Noakes to bring over anything of yours, and that applies to the London flat equally. I think perhaps it might be a good idea if we collect Lucky at the weekends and he can stay here with you. We can drop him off on our way back on Monday mornings.' He paused to think. 'Better still, supposing I have him over here permanently? I've two dogs; another one won't make any difference. He can come here whenever you're staying the night.'

'Oh, could he? I shall miss him, but I'm sure he'd be happy with you.'

'You flatter me.' The mockery in his voice sent the colour into her cheeks; he watched it fade before saying, 'That's settled. I'll take you back.'

She could think of nothing to say once they were back in the car. She sensed that chatter about her new job would irritate him; as far as he was concerned the whole business was cut and dried and there was no need to mull it over. Only, as he stopped the car outside her old home, he suggested, 'I'll send you a letter confirming the job, and give you dates and so on.'

She had no chance to do more than nod as they went into the house and Mrs Culver opened the drawing-room door. 'Ralph—how nice! Come in, dear, and have a drink—stay to dinner if you can.' She smiled at Meg. 'I'm sure Meg can do something about that.'

'Yes, of course, Mrs Culver.' She went, still in her outdoor things, to the kitchen, where she found Betsy putting the finishing touches to duckling and black cherry sauce.

'You look as though you could do with a cup of tea, Miss Meg. Just you wait a jiffy—the kettle's on the boil.' Betsy bustled around making the tea. 'I can see you're bursting with news, love, but I'll 'ave ter wait, won't I?'

Meg sipped the tea, stooped to fondle Lucky and Silky and took off her coat. 'Oh, I've lots to tell you, Betsy! But I think the Professor's staying for dinner—can we manage or shall I open a tin or two?' She looked up as one of the old-fashioned bells on the kitchen wall jangled. 'That's the drawing-room; I'll see what's wanted.'

When she went in Mrs Culver was sitting in her usual chair and the Professor was standing with an arm on the mantelpiece, staring into the fire. He put his glass down as she crossed the room. 'I'm not staying for dinner, Meg.' He gave his mother an apologetic smile. 'I've a date this evening, my dear.'

'Is she very beautiful?' Mrs Culver chuckled.

'Very. And she doesn't like to be kept waiting.' He put down his glass, kissed her and went to the door. 'I'll send you the details, Meg. Don't bother to see me out.'

The rest of the evening was spent in discussing the details of Meg's new job. 'Really—it's providential!' declared Mrs Culver. 'Tell me, dear, what was this London flat like? Ralph thought nothing of it . . .'

Presently, on the plea of helping Betsy wash up and prepare for the morning, Meg told her old friend what had happened.

Betsy nodded her head. 'As was to be expected,' she observed. 'I 'ad a feeling that all would come right. A pity as 'ow yer've got to work in London, but yer'll be near enough at the weekends—we'll see each other now and then, I've no doubt. 'Ave yer told yer sisters, Miss Meg?'

'Not yet. It's a bit late to do it now; I'll phone them in the morning.'

She rang Cora first and found little opposition, 'Well, if that's what you want to do, Meg. I suppose you can buy a place later on. I must say it'll be a relief to have you settled at last, at least for a time. What's the flat like that you'll take over?'

'I haven't seen it . . .'

Cora sounded huffy. 'Well, you know your own business best, I suppose. If you choose to ignore Doreen and me that's your affair.'

Meg agreed quietly that it was and then hung up. Doreen answered the phone with something of a snap. 'Meg, you know I don't like you ringing up when I'm on duty. If it's something to do with the flat . . .'

Meg told her and then listened to Doreen's voice

pointing out all the drawbacks. 'What's come over you?' she wanted to know. 'You've always done what Cora and I have suggested, and now here you are going off on a wild-goose chase . . . Well, I suppose you'll do what you want.' She added, 'Once you're settled in I'll come and see you. Does Professor Culver live over his rooms?'

'No, there's only a caretaker and his wife. I don't know where he lives.'

Doreen said thoughtfully, 'You'll be able to find out. We got on rather well together when we met . . .' She rang off and Meg, relieved that her sisters had been only mildly annoyed, looked for Lucky and took him for a walk and then cycled into Hertingfordbury to give Mrs Grimes the weekly order; Mrs Culver believed in supporting the local tradespeople.

She received a letter from the Professor the following day—very businesslike, setting out her duties and the conditions concerning her job, and directing that she was to go to town with Noakes in three days' time so that she might see the flat and be taken over the consulting rooms and meet his secretary and the receptionist whose place she was to take.

She showed the letter to Mrs Culver, who read it through and then observed comfortably that Ralph would see to everything and she was to do as he suggested. 'And when you want to go over to the cottage at Much Hadham, just let me know, dear, so that Noakes can take you.' She glanced at the letter again. 'Ralph suggests that you start work in two weeks. That fits very nicely; Kate comes here two days earlier and you'll be able to show her the house and see that she knows where everything is. Were your sisters pleased?'

Meg folded her letter carefully. 'Rather surprised, but—well, relieved that I would be settled. I only hope I'll be satisfactory.'

Mrs Culver smiled. 'Ralph never makes mistakes; if

he decided that you'll be good in the job, then you will be.' She spoke with a firm conviction which bolstered up Meg's dubious second thoughts.

It was teeming with rain as Noakes and Meg left three days later. There had been no help for it but to wear her elderly Burberry and tie a scarf over her hair. Hardly what she would have chosen to wear on a trip to London, but she assumed that once she had paid her visit to the consulting rooms and seen the flat she would have to find her way to the station and take a train back. No one had said anything about the return journey, and she could hardly ask Noakes. Perhaps he would mention it on the way.

He didn't; she got out, a bundle of nerves, when he drew up before an elegant, narrow house in a terrace of similar houses in a tree-lined street, bade him goodbye, and rang the highly polished bell by the front door.

It opened and she went inside to find a surprisingly roomy hall with several handsome mahogany doors and a graceful staircase ahead of her. The door nearest her had 'Reception' written above it, so she opened it and went in. It was a pleasant room and she had the impression of neutral shades tinged with amber as she crossed the thick carpet to the desk in one corner.

The young woman sitting behind it was pretty, and she had a nice smile. She said now, 'You're Meg Collins, aren't you? Professor Culver told us you would be coming. He's not here at present—it's his morning at Maud's—but I'm to show you round. Miss Standish, his secretary, will come in here while I'm away. Would you like a cup of coffee? There won't be any patients until two o'clock.' She got up, and Meg saw that she was quite tall and slim and elegantly dressed; she would have to buy clothes, she thought worriedly, very conscious of the Burberry.

'I'm Rosalind Adams,' the girl added. 'Do sit down

and I'll get the coffee.'

She disappeared through a door behind the desk and reappeared almost at once with a tray with cups and saucers and a percolator.

Meg took a heartening sip from the cup handed to her. 'I'm scared,' she admitted. 'I've never worked in an office before.'

'Well, this isn't quite like an office. Professor Culver believes that people who come here for consultation need to feel reassured, so it's more like paying a visit, if you see what I mean. The work's easy: making appointments, writing them up, checking patients as they come, going to the Post Office, making tea and coffee and doing odd jobs. The difficult part is knowing what to say to the patients; you know, being sympathetic, or bracing, or impersonal. It's a kind of instinct, and if the Professor offered you the job you'll have got it, so you've no need to worry.' Rosalind sounded quite sure about it, and Meg began to feel better. Presently Miss Standish, cosily middle-aged and not at all the kind of secretary Meg would have supposed the Professor to have, came in, made a few kindly remarks and sat down at the desk as Rosalind ushered Meg back into the hall and up the stairs. The first floor was given over to treatment rooms, a cloakroom, a miniature kitchen for making tea and a second consulting room, and the floor above that was the flat. It had its own front door, opening on to a lobby with three doors. 'Sitting-room,' said Rosalind, flinging open one of them and disclosing a pleasant room with a small window at the front and glass doors leading to a balcony at the back. It was nicely furnished with a couple of easy chairs in cretonne covers, matching curtains, a small table and two chairs, bookshelves on either side of a small gas fire, and a television in one corner.

Rosalind whisked back into the lobby and opened the door opposite. 'Bedroom—a bit small.'

It had a sloping roof and window at the front. Small it might be, but it was pretty too, with a flowery wallpaper and a white-painted bed and furniture, and a door in the far wall opened into a very small bathroom, tiled in pale pink.

'Kitchen,' said Rosalind, back in the lobby, and opened the last door, Another small room with a door leading to a balcony, with everything in it that one might need.

Meg breathed a deep sigh. 'It's super; I had no idea . . . do you mean to say that I can live here?'

'Goes with the job. Mind you, you'll get disturbed by the phone and have to pass messages on and so on—not everyone's cup of tea, but I've been here for years and loved it. If I hadn't been going to marry I dare say I'd have gone on for ever. As you know, there's a caretaker and his wife—they live in the basement, and he'll do little jobs for you if you need help. Come down and see the consulting room; I'll show you where everything is so that you won't feel too lost.'

It was behind the reception room with a wide window overlooking a narrow walled garden at the back of the house. It had a massive desk covered untidily with papers and folders, two or three comfortable chairs and heavy silk curtains at the windows. There was a little rosewood wall table opposite the desk with a bowl of pink chrysanthemums on it, and the carpet was thick and soft. A door at one side led to Miss Standish's office. 'Of course, you don't come in here often,' explained Rosalind, 'just to collect the post or take a message or usher in a patient. I'll be here for a couple of days when you start, and you'll pick everything up quickly enough.'

'I do hope so. I'll have to buy the right kind of clothes.' Meg looked at her companion's plain blue dress, well cut and elegant.

'Yes—well, the Professor's against overalls and so on.

He has a nurse, of course—she's in uniform and comes for consulting hours—but I wear navy blue or grey, either a dress or a skirt and plain blouse.'

They went back to the reception room and Miss Standish trotted off with the remark that she was looking forward to having Meg working with her. 'Oh, and Professor Culver telephoned—you're to be here at four o'clock and he'll drive you back.' She glanced at her watch. 'Lots of time for you to do some shopping if you want to.'

'Why not?' thought Meg, suddenly light-hearted. Armed with useful information about buses and a suitable café for a snack lunch, she bade a temporary goodbye and went to the nearest bus stop.

She was back just before four o'clock with a carrier bag containing a navy blue dress in wool crêpe with a white collar and a demure bow. It had cost quite a lot of money, but nothing less would have done for the quiet luxury of the consulting rooms. It was practical too, for the collar was detachable and she had bought several more in different colours. She had bought shoes—plain black courts—and sheer stockings, and once she was living in the flat she would add to her wardrobe and see that it was adequate; she hadn't realised until now just how dowdy she had become.

Rosalind gave her a cup of tea and took one in to Miss Standish, and they were tidying the cups and saucers away when the Professor arrived. He gave her a brief nod, gave Rosalind a handful of envelopes and went to his consulting room.

'I post these on the way home,' said Rosalind. 'If he's got patients here we usually work until five or six o'clock, and most Saturday mornings too. Miss Standish and I take it in turns to take a few hours off to make up for that.'

The Professor came out of his room then, wished Miss

Standish and Rosalind a good day, and swept Meg before him out to the car.

She was still feeling light-hearted. She said shyly, 'The flat is lovely, Professor Culver.' And when he grunted in reply, she added, 'I think I shall like working for you; I hope . . . I'll do my best.'

'You won't stay long if you don't!' He sounded so unfriendly that she decided not to say another word until he did. Only he didn't; not a word was said until he stopped outside his mother's front door. 'Thank you for the lift, Professor Culver,' said Meg clearly; her voice held a volume of feeling and his stern mouth relaxed. If he had been going to say anything, she didn't give him the chance; she darted indoors, whisked into the drawing-room to tell Mrs Culver that she was back and went to the kitchen, where she shed her coat, kicked off her shoes and sat down at the table where Betsy was rolling pastry.

'Well?' said her old friend. 'Everything nicely settled, Miss Meg?'

'Oh, yes, Betsy. It's a lovely flat, and the place where I'm to work is very upper crust. I wish I'd never said I'd take the job . . .'

Betsy finished putting little dabs of butter on her pastry and folding it carefully before she observed, 'You're tired, love, and think of that lovely little cottage; if I can manage it, I'll come over on me Sunday, 'alf day.'

'Oh, Betsy, will you? I'll love that.' Meg twiddled Lucky's ears. 'I'll have him, too.' She got up. 'I'd better tidy myself and go to Mrs Culver. I must let Doreen and Cora know when I'm moving.'

When she went to the drawing-room ten minutes later, Professor Culver had gone. 'He couldn't stay,' said Mrs Culver with regret. 'He has two consultations this evening. Do you feel you can be happy in that little flat, Meg?'

'Oh, yes, it's lovely.' It struck Meg that the Professor hadn't asked her if she had liked it, nor, to give him his due, had he evinced any desire for gratitude on her part. 'I think I shall be very happy there.'

'I do hope so, my dear. I shall miss you . . . Kate comes tomorrow; I shall leave you to show her round and settle her in and of course you must come and see me whenever you can—and see Betsy too. She will miss you so.'

'Yes, but at least she's not being uprooted—she's been here for such a long time, I think it would have killed her . . .'

'Well, dear, you may be sure that she will stay here for the rest of her days. She'll be such a support for Kate.'

'You think they'll get on?'

'I'm sure they will.'

When Kate arrived, Meg thought that probably Mrs Culver was right. Kate was tall, thin and unassuming. Her voice was quiet and her manner retiring, and she professed herself delighted with the house, her room and Betsy. Moreover, she took instantly to the elderly and cunning Silky, who lost no time in ingratiating himself. Meg left the two women gossiping happily over a pot of tea in the kitchen and went upstairs to pack her treasures in the boxes Noakes would take to the flat for her. While she did it she mulled over her sisters' reactions. Cora was annoyed because she hadn't taken her advice, but all the same she was relieved. 'You can always come here when you get your holidays,' she had invited. 'I only hope the job lasts.'

Doreen had been even more annoyed, largely because Meg had taken such an important step without relying on her sister's considered advice. But that annoyance too had been tempered with a thinly veiled curiosity about Professor Culver. 'I dare say I shall see more of him, for of course I shall keep an eye on you, darling.' She could almost hear Doreen thinking. 'And that dear little cottage for the weekends—how very kind he is—I must thank him when I see him!'

'I've done that,' said Meg with unwonted tartness.

Noakes took her over the next day to the cottage, with her bits of furniture sticking out of the boot, and helped her to carry them in and arrange them; there wasn't much: a little work table of her mother's, a few pictures and a little prayer chair, and a few books. The rest were to go to the flat in London, and the village carrier had undertaken to deliver those before she got there. She had been careful to arrange for their delivery in the evening after everyone had gone home, when only the caretaker was there.

She spent the next two days showing Kate around and initiating her into the daily routine. 'Though I dare say you'll alter things to suit yourself.' said Meg politely. 'You'll find Betsy a great help, and there's Mrs Griffiths who comes in from the village and is very good—she's been coming for years.' She cast a quick glance and saw Kate's feet in roomy felt slippers. 'You're sure you feel well enough to manage? Mrs Griffiths is going to do an extra day each week . . .'

'Bless you, miss; I'll be all right. That Betsy knows the place back to front, and I'm sure we're going to like each other. And the house almost runs itself, doesn't it? Nice place it is too, after that flat in Amsterdam.'

'Amsterdam?' queried Meg.

'Well, Mrs Culver's mother is Dutch—when her husband died she went back there to live and naturally Mrs Culver pays her long visits, especially now she's lost her own husband. It's a lovely flat, mind you, far too large for the old lady, but there, it was her home when she was a child and she refuses to leave it. Verging on ninety, too—the Professor's very fond of her.'

The idea of Professor Culver having a granny struck Meg as surprising, somehow he didn't seem much of a family man. She murmured a suitable reply to this interesting bit of information and offered to show Kate the stock of jams and bottled fruit, kept in a chilly little room leading off the kitchen. 'Pickled apricots,' said Kate admiringly, 'spiced oranges—you're a good house-wife, if I may say so, miss. The Professor's granny would take to you—a great one she is with jams and pickles, or she was when she was younger. She'd spend hours bottling fruit and such ... mind you, there was always someone to clear up afterwards.'

The two days went pleasantly, and on the third morning Meg bade everyone farewell, got into the car beside Noakes and was whisked away to London. She had hated leaving Lucky. Noakes was taking him over to Much Hadham that evening and she would see him at the weekend. But before that there was almost a whole week to get through ...

Four days later she had to admit that she had enjoyed every moment of them. She had seen practically nothing of Professor Culver; for a good bit of the day he wasn't there, anyway, and when he was, she only glimpsed him at his desk as she ushered his patients in or took in his tea or coffee. He had paused once on his way out to ask if she had settled in, and when she had told him yes, he had nodded and gone away without a word. Rosalind had been very kind, nudging her into doing the right thing, explaining good-temperedly about the patients, writing out a timetable of her work, going with her to the Post Office, showing her where the spare keys were kept and how to manage the intercom and the small switchboard. The Professor had been right; there was nothing complicated about the job. All one needed was a willingness to work hard, and not watch the clock, and the ability to make tea or coffee at a moment's notice. She hadn't a great deal to do with the patients yet, but now that Rosalind had gone, she would see rather more of them, although Miss Standish dealt with all the major enquiries.

She had enjoyed making herself at home in the flat. With her own small possessions scattered around, it took on a cosy familiarity which was most satisfying to return to at the end of the day's work. And on Saturday she would be going to the cottage and would see Lucky again.

Doreen had phoned; she would come and see Meg one evening the following week, she said, and she asked casually if the Professor was ever there in the evenings. 'Never,' said Meg. 'I've a number I switch calls to; I suppose it's his home or the hospital.' Doreen had seemed disappointed.

It was quiet once everyone had gone; Meg had been sorry to see Rosalind's elegant back disappearing through the street door. She called good night to the caretaker, shut the door and went up to her flat. It looked delightful in the soft light of a table lamp, the curtains drawn against the dusk outside and the gas fire glowing. She went into the kitchen and put a lamb chop under the grill; she used her lunch hour in which to shop and made do with coffee and a sandwich, for cooking in the evenings gave her something to do. In a few days when she was thoroughly at home, she would go for a brisk walk before she got her supper, and of course in the summer she would be able to sit on the balcony.

Supper eaten, she wrote a letter to Mrs Culver and another one to Betsy, and since her kitchen bin was full and the caretaker wouldn't be along to empty it until the end of the week, she tied the plastic bag neatly, took her key and went downstairs to the side door on the ground floor which opened on to the square of paving stones where the bins were kept. There were four of them; she put her bag into the last of them and was on the point of going back indoors when something caught her eye. A bedraggled cat, sitting uneasily against the brick wall, watching her. The light over the door shone on to his face; he was one-eyed and had tattered ears. He sat and made no sound, and Meg went slowly towards him and picked him up. He was feather-light, skin and bones, and she exclaimed in pity. Without stopping to consider the matter, she carried him up to her flat where she sat him down in front of the fire and fetched a saucer of milk. He lapped it up with pathetic speed and she gave him more, this time with bread soaked in it. He scoffed that too, and crept nervously back towards the fire, to turn and slink under her chair as she arranged a cushion on the floor. 'Well, it was a bit lonely,' she told him, 'and if you care to stay, you're more than welcome, for I'm sure you've no home of your own.'

She sat down and kept quite still until presently he crept out again and sat down on the cushion. 'It'll be nice to have someone to talk to.' Meg went on, 'but you'll have to fit in with me—no going out, just the balcony, but if you're good I'll take you to the cottage each weekend.'

The cat stared at her with his one eye and presently went to sleep, which gave her the chance to go downstairs to the caretaker and beg an old wooden box from him. There was a flower bed in the back garden, and she shovelled earth and went back upstairs and put the box on the balcony, and then went back to look at the cat. He was awake again, watching her warily, and she offered more food, and this time he purred wheezily.

By the time she had showered and got ready for bed he had explored the flat, investigated the balcony and returned to his cushion. She put yet another saucer of milk down on the kitchen floor, wished him a good night and got into bed. She hadn't shut her bedroom door; she was almost asleep when he crept on to the bed and arranged himself on her feet. He was grubby, to say the least, but she was grateful for his company.

He got up when she did, ate the breakfast she gave him

and sat down on the cushion and began rather half-heartedly to wash himself. Meg left the door on to the balcony open and went down to the consulting rooms to begin her day's work. The cat had given her a worried look when she had gone to the door, and she had told him hearteningly that she would be back in an hour or two. Tomorrow, she thought happily, I'll be going to the cottage; he can come too. He could travel in a cardboard box—there were plenty in the basement—but she would have to ask the Professor if he minded. She thrust the thought to the back of her mind and started on her chores, making sure that the waiting-room was just so, arranging the daily papers and magazines on the two or three tables, getting out the coffee percolator, freshening the flowers, opening the windows and lastly getting out the case notes. There weren't very many; the Professor always went to Maud's at half past eleven on Friday mornings and didn't get back until his first afternoon appointment.

She had remembered everything. Miss Standish, arriving half an hour later, expressed her satisfaction, rearranged her stylish hairdo and drank the tea Meg had made for her. Five minutes later the Professor arrived, gave her an austere good morning and went into his consulting room. Meg, going in with his coffee, saw that he was already deep in his post, with Miss Standish, enviably efficient, sitting close by, notebook and pencil at the ready.

There was a brief wait for the first patient; Meg drank the rest of Miss Standish's tea and arranged herself at the desk. At least she looked the part in her blue dress.

The first two patients were elderly, come for their regular check-ups, and they were familiar with the procedure and knew what was expected of them without being told. The nurse, with a cheeful nod at Meg, had fetched them in their turn, and after short intervals they

returned to make appointments for their next visits. Meg
ushered them out with suitable murmurs and looked at
the appointments book. One more: a Mrs Denver.

The girl who walked in didn't look old enough to be
Mrs anyone. She was tall and slim, exquisitely dressed
and made-up; she was in the kind of clothes models wore.
Meg smiled at her as she crossed to the desk and saw then
that the girl was shaking with fright. With luck the nurse
would come quickly, thought Meg, being politely
welcoming and asking the girl to take a seat. She looked
so wretched that Meg began on a mild chat about the
weather, to be interrupted by her companion.

'I don't believe it,' she declared in a voice squeaky with
nerves. 'They make mistakes, don't they? These clever
professors think they know everything! I don't feel ill,
and I don't see why I should have to come here—they
said I might have to go to hospital!' She shuddered
strongly. 'Well, I won't and no one can make me. I told
my husband so.' She looked as though she was going to
cry. 'He couldn't come with me. What's he like, this
Professor Culver?'

'You'll like him,' said Meg promptly. 'He's kind, very
clever and everyone likes him.' She wasn't sure if she
should discuss him with a patient, but Rosalind hadn't
said anything about it. It was a relief when the nurse
came to fetch Mrs Denver.

She was in the consulting room for a long time, and
half-way through Meg was asked on the intercom to take
in a cup of coffee for the patient. Mrs Denver was white
under her make-up; she was sitting in the chair facing
Professor Culver's desk, and the nurse was standing
beside her. The Professor said, 'Thank you, Meg,'
without looking at her, and she went back to the waiting-
room, tidied it and got out the case sheets for the
afternoon patients. It struck her forcibly that she would
have to learn something of the Professor's work; she read

the case sheets and made little or no sense of them. To understand them, she would have to get hold of a book about radiology and what it was all about. There were lots of books in the consulting room; when everyone had gone home she would take her pick and study the subject. Mrs Denver, escorted by the nurse, came back presently.

'You were quite right,' she told Meg. 'He is awfully kind.' She looked as though she was going to cry. 'I'm going into Maud's and he'll look after me.' She turned to leave. 'You've got a nice little face,' she told an astounded Meg. 'Motherly, if you know what I mean.'

The nurse came back, smiling. 'We haven't met,' she said. 'I'm Mary Giles, and you're Meg, aren't you? I'm not always here—I'm going off now as soon as the Professor's gone—but I come in again this afternoon. Do you think you're going to like it here?'

'Yes,' said Meg, and she meant it.

She went upstairs for her snack lunch later, locking up carefully before she went. The cat was sitting on the balcony; he looked cleaner but he was woefully thin. She gave him a heaped saucer of food—cheese and bits of bacon and bread in milk—and he gobbled the lot. There was no time to go to the shops for cat food; she would ask the caretaker if he would get it for her. She hadn't quite got her shopping organised yet. She made coffee and sandwiches for herself, loaded the saucer again and went to see the caretaker. A fat little man—always cheerful. 'Got a cat, 'ave you?' He beamed at her. 'Make a bit of company evenings, like, won't it? I'll put the stuff outside yer door, 'fore I go down to the pub for 'arf an hour.'

The afternoon went smoothly. The last patient had gone by four o'clock, and the Professor followed him almost at once. Beyond telling Meg to phone him at the number he'd left, and wishing her a cool good afternoon, he had nothing to say. Miss Standish went shortly afterwards, and Meg, left on her own, wondered if he had forgotten his offer of a lift the next day. But she didn't waste time worrying about that; she went to the consulting room, chose what she hoped was a suitable book on radiology, locked up, and then went up to her flat. She fed the cat, made tea, and with him curled up beside her on her chair, began to read. It was all way above her head but absorbing; she had quite forgotten where she was. When there was a knock on the door she called 'Come in,' without even taking her eyes off the book.

CHAPTER FIVE

IT was Professor Culver who came in and paused in the open door of the sitting-room. He began politely, 'I'm sorry to disturb you, Meg, I came back to fetch a book from my consulting room but it isn't on its usual shelf. Perhaps you've seen it? Miss Standish may have had it.'

Meg had got to her feet, the book in her hand, one finger marking the open page. 'Is this it?' she asked helpfully.

He strode towards her, bringing with him such a circumjacence of rage that she took a step backwards.

'Ah, so you have it—I wasn't aware that I'd made you free of the books in my consulting room.' He spoke softly, but she would rather that he had shouted at her; he had the look of an angry man.

He took the book from her and at the same time saw the cat, staring at him one-eyed from her chair. He said in the same soft voice, 'And what is that bedraggled creature doing here, filthy dirty and no doubt flea-ridden?' His black eyes narrowed and his mouth had a nasty curl to it. 'Have you not got a little above yourself, my girl? Helping yourself to my books, bringing verminous animals into this house . . .' He was getting really cross; it was time to stop him before he was in a real rage.

'One animal,' she corrected him in a reasonable voice, 'and although he's starved and dirty he is not verminous. I dare say if you had to live from hand to mouth among the dustbins you would be dirty and probably flea-ridden too. I shall take good care of him, and in a few weeks' time you won't know him.' She returned his dark look with an almost motherly smile. 'And there's really no need to be so cross,' and at his outraged snort, 'well, you are, you know—it can't be good for you. I'm sorry I took the book without asking you first, but you see, now that I've been working here for a few days it seems to me that I don't know a thing about your work—that Mrs Denver who came this morning, she was so frightened and I couldn't comfort her because I didn't understand what was wrong with her—I mean, she could have had a broken rib or TB or something, couldn't she? And you're a radiologist, and that's X-rays, isn't it?' She looked at him hopefully. 'You see what I mean, Professor Culver?'

'Your grammar is deplorable, but I get the gist of your remarks. I must tell you that TB is seldom encountered these days, and I don't have much to do with broken bones. I work with radium, either as X-rays or radioactive substances; they're used for the treatment or cure of malignant diseases, either on their own or combined with surgery. I have no intention of going into the matter deeply with you, but since you're interested I'll let you have a book which explains the work we do. If you'll come with me I'll get it for you.

'And may I keep the cat?' she added with unconscious wistfulness. 'He's company, you know. Someone to talk to.'

He turned away to open the door. 'Provided that he stays here. What do you intend to do with him at weekends?'

'If I may put him in a box . . . would you mind if he came in the car with me?'

'And supposing that I mind?'

'Well, you didn't mind about Lucky?'

'Hoist with my own petard! I've no option, have I? Bring the beast.'

'Thank you.' Meg preceded him down to the consulting room and waited quietly while he found the book which she was to have. He made no attempt at any further conversation, merely gave it to her and wished her an indifferent good night.

It wasn't that he disliked her, thought Meg, going slowly upstairs again, it was complete indifference. She doubted if he had looked at her for more than a couple of seconds. In the flat she delivered a short lecture to the cat on the subject of behaving himself in the car.

His behaviour was excellent; he sat in his box, not moving, his eye on the road ahead. After a little while Meg, in the front beside the Professor, stopped sitting with her head over one shoulder anxiously watching his every move, and relaxed. It was an unexpectedly spring-like day, and the country, once they reached it, was giving a hint of better weather to come. The Professor hardly spoke, but by now Meg had reconciled herself to his lack of interest; she had so much to be thankful for, she reminded herself robustly: a job, a cosy little home in the best part of London and the bonus of a weekend cottage in the country. She didn't think that that would last long, but while it did she was going to enjoy it.

They were going through Much Hadham before the Professor said, 'I shall be driving back tomorrow evening. Please be ready by half past six. I'll stop outside the lodge.'

He slowed the car, and she was surprised when he got out and carried the cat's box into the cottage for her. 'Lucky will be brought down very shortly,' he told her, and got back into the car and drove on. Her thanks, half said, died on her lips.

'Rude,' said Meg, and forgot him in the pleasure of being at the cottage. She had brought food and milk and tea with her, and presently she would walk into Much Hadham and stock up with something of everything. There was a small fridge in the kitchen, and an old-fashioned pantry. She fed the cat and allowed him to

roam through the little place, although he showed no
wish to go outside. There hadn't been time to eat lunch
before they left, so she made tea and cut a hunk of bread
from the loaf and munched and swallowed as she put the
little place to rights. There were logs outside the back
door; she laid a fire in the sitting-room and, with the cat
sitting on the open window sill, went into the garden. As
soon as Lucky came, she could go to the shops; in the
meantime she was happy enough to inspect the flower
beds.

She was crouching on her heels admiring a clump of
primroses half hidden by the hedge when she heard a car.
The professor, going the other way with Lucky sitting in
the back.

Meg went to the little wooden gate and opened the car
door. Lucky shot out, overjoyed to see her, and the
Professor said, 'I'll fetch him back before we leave
tomorrow,' and raised a hand as he drove off.

The animals didn't object to each other; beyond a few
minutes of wary scrutiny, they seemed prepared to accept
the situation. Meg found a length of rope to tie to Lucky's
collar, shut the doors and windows and set off with her
shopping basket and the dog.

It was marvellous to be in the country again, and after
a week of wearing her sober navy dress, it was a nice
change to wear a tweed skirt and a thick sweater. She
walked briskly, towed by Lucky, did her shopping and
started off home again. She was almost there when the
Rolls passed her, and this time there was a girl sitting
beside the Professor. Meg, who had splendid eyesight,
could see that she was very pretty; she was laughing at
the Professor too, tossing golden hair off her shoulders.
She glanced at Meg as they went by, an indifferent look
which took in the elderly sweater and sensible shoes. The
Professor raised his hand again but he didn't look at her.
The girl looked back, and Meg guessed she had wanted to

know who she was. 'Well, she needn't worry,' she told
Lucky, 'there's absolutely no competition.'

Which set her thinking. It would be nice to provide
that competition, but how? How to attract the Professor's attention, get him to be interested in her, even to fall
for her? She was quite shocked at the idea, for she was
hopelessly out-of-date in her views. She liked the idea of
getting married and having children; she even believed it
was possible to live happily ever after. The Professor was
hardly the man she would choose to fulfil these hopes. On
the other hand, he could do with a lesson; just because
she was plain and a nonentity it didn't mean that she had
to stay that way.

She reached the cottage, fed the animals and sat down
to think. He was a tiresome man, accustomed to having
his own way and ill-tempered when he didn't get it. On
the other hand he was kind. A good wife could turn him
into something quite different.

She made tea, lit the fire and presently busied herself
getting supper. When she had eaten it, she sat down by
the fire again with Lucky at her feet and the cat squashed
between them. 'I must give you a name,' she told him.
'Something rather splendid to make up for only having
one eye.' She reflected for a few minutes. 'Nelson,' she
declared.

She slept dreamlessly, lulled by the quiet around the
cottage, and then spent a happy day poking round the
garden; there was a lot to be done, for it had been
neglected throughout the winter. None the less there
were green shoots poking up amongst the weeds and
dead leaves. After her lunch she left Nelson in front of
the fire and took Lucky for a walk. She had tea early and
packed her bag and set the cottage to rights. She was
bringing in logs, ready for the following weekend, when
the Rolls went whispering past with Professor Culver
and his pretty companion. She was cleaning the grate

ready for laying a fire when he returned and stopped
outside, this time alone. She whistled to Lucky and went
out to the gate. 'He's had his tea,' she observed, and
popped him into the back of the car. She gave the
Professor a pleasant smile. 'I'm quite ready when you
want to go.'

He said slowly, 'Have you had tea? Come up to the
house and have it with me.'

She said gently, 'Thank you, but I've had my tea.'
Then added kindly, 'Besides, I expect you've had it
already.'

He looked surprised as he drove off.

Meg was ready and waiting for him when he came
back, standing at the gate with Nelson dozing in his box,
and she got into the car without fuss while he saw to the
bag and the cat. They had passed Much Hadham and
were on the main road before he spoke.

'You've enjoyed your weekend, Meg?'

'Yes, thank you. Very much.'

He glanced sideways at her, expecting her to say more.
'You have all you need in the cottage?'

'Yes, thank you.'

His firm mouth twitched with amusement. 'Has the
cat got your tongue, Meg?'

'Certainly not.' She sounded matter-of-fact. 'I can't
think of anything interesting to talk about, and I think
you dislike chatter.'

He drove in silence for a while. 'Now what have I done
or said to deserve such severity? Are you disliking the
idea of going back to work?'

'Not a bit—I'm quite looking forward to it. I read the
book you lent me and now I'm reading it again, just to
make sure that I understood it.

'What else do you do, Meg? Besides reading and
gardening and rescuing animals? Theatre? Concerts?
Dancing, dining out . . .?'

'Well, I haven't been out much; I expect I like all those things, though.'

He glanced at her serene little face again but didn't say anything. The rest of the journey was passed in silence, and when they got to the consulting rooms, although he carried Nelson upstairs for her and waited while she unlocked the door, he merely wished her good night, ignoring her thanks.

Meg settled Nelson before the fire and went to get their supper. She hoped she hadn't been too offhand with the Professor, but at least she had startled him a bit. This week, she decided, she would speak when spoken to, do her work to perfection and take great care not to annoy him in any way. Of course, he might not even notice, and she would fade into even greater obscurity but what would that matter? Right at the back of her head was the nagging thought that he wasn't as happy as he ought to be; he had money, work he obviously enjoyed, he was good-looking and doubtless had any number of friends and could take his pick of pretty girls, so what else did he want? A wife, said Meg to Nelson, who winked back at her. 'Someone like me.' The idea was so preposterous that she burst out laughing.

All the same, she went down to start work on Monday morning determined to keep to her plan. She was sitting demurely at her desk by the time the Professor arrived; she had done all her small chores, given Miss Standish her tea and had the coffee ready to pour. She wished him good morning and gave him the sort of smile she imagined a receptionist would give a distinguished consultant. Presently she went into his room and put his coffee down on the desk beside him and slipped out again soundlessly. He looked up from his letter to watch her disappear through the door, a faint frown between his eyes. He frowned several times during the day too. Meg seemed different; she had become a shadow of herself, so self-effacing that he found himself watching her, something he hadn't done before. He had begun, unconsciously, to expect her direct way of talking, her matter-of-fact manner, her flashes of temper, just as he had taken for granted the rather dull life she led. He still didn't know why he had offered her a job and the lodge; he had done it on the spur of the moment and had been sorry about it afterwards, although he had been agreeably surprised to find that she was everything that he expected of someone working for him.

At the end of a busy afternoon, on his way out, he stopped to ask her if she felt all right.

'Oh, I'm very well, thank you Professor Culver.' She smiled, 'Good night.'

After he had gone, she took the post, locked up and went upstairs to get her outdoor things. The Post Office was five minutes' walk away, and she enjoyed the short trip each evening. There were quite a few people about, going home or going out for the evening; she wouldn't admit to herself that she was lonely, but she felt less so with people hurrying to and fro around her. It could have been far worse, she told herself; she could have been living in that dreadful flat behind Waterloo Station with some dreary job and no lovely weekends at Much Hadham. She stopped to talk to Percy the caretaker as she went indoors, and let herself into her flat, feeling cheerful again. Quite a bit of the evening was taken up cooking her supper, and twice she had to switch the phone through to the Professor's house. She was getting ready for bed when Doreen rang to say that she would be round on the following evening. 'About seven o'clock,' she said. 'Will Professor Culver be there?'

'He goes about five o'clock, sometimes later if there's a patient, but tomorrow he's at Maud's in the afternoon and he doesn't come back.'

Doreen sounded disappointed. 'Oh, well, I'll come just

the same,' she told Meg tactlessly, and rang off without asking her how she was getting on.

She arrived punctually and was instantly aggrieved because Meg wouldn't unlock the waiting-room door and let her look round. 'You are silly!' she said, half angrily. 'As though it matters! There's nobody there—I only want to look.'

'I'll ask Professor Culver if he minds, and next time you come perhaps we can go in. But not now. Come upstairs: I've got supper ready.'

Doreen was impressed by the flat. 'Why, it's delightful—you lucky girl!' She saw Nelson in his box. 'What on earth have you got there?'

Meg explained and Doreen laughed. 'You always were a funny little thing, finding animals and persuading half the village to give them homes. You like looking after people too, don't you? You coped with Mother beautifully.'

Meg didn't answer that. 'Sit down, Doreen. I've got some sherry—we'll have it before I dish up.'

'When do you shop?' asked Doreen.

'Well, there's just about time during the lunch hour, only I have to look sharp about it.'

'Did you go to this marvellous cottage you were telling us about?'

'Yes, it was so lovely—I had Lucky with me and Nelson came down too.'

'Did Professor Culver give you a lift?'

'Yes. He has to pass the door to get to his home.'

'What's it like, his home?'

'I don't know . . .'

'Meg, you're hopeless! Didn't you go and explore?'

'I never thought about it. Anyway it would be a bit rude, wouldn't it? I didn't see it the first time we went down to the cottage.'

Over supper Doreen asked, 'Do you get on with him well, Meg?'

'I work for him.' said Meg soberly. 'We don't—don't socialise.'

Doreen laughed. 'Any other girl would be making the most of her chances,' she observed. 'He'd be quite a catch.'

'Well, I think he's caught. There was a very pretty girl there this weekend. Just the kind of girl one would imagine he would marry . . .'

'So you think about him?' Doreen observed slyly.

Meg passed the vegetables. 'As an employer, yes—I expect you think about the doctors you work for? I don't know anything about him—his private life—and I don't particularly want to.' Which wasn't quite true. Moreover, she didn't want to talk about him.

Doreen's flat proved a splendid red herring; she described it at length, saying rather casually that when Meg was free she must come and spend an evening with her. 'Though I go out a great deal and I suppose you like to have a bit of peace and quiet at the end of the day.'

Meg got to up to switch a call through to the Professor's house. 'Yes, I do, and I have to be here to take phone calls, though the caretaker will do it if I want to go out. As long as it's not too often.'

'Well, you don't know anyone, do you?' Doreen accepted ice cream. 'I must say Cora and I are surprised that you've fallen on your feet. We don't need to worry about you any more, thank goodness.'

Meg didn't say anything to that. She loved her sisters, but there was no getting away from the fact that when their mother had become ill, they had taken it for granted that she should be the one to stay at home and nurse her. In all fairness, she supposed that if she had been one or other of them, she might have done the same. She would have liked to explain to Doreen that even though she had

this good job and a little home to go with it, she would
have preferred to have stayed in Hertingfordbury. But
that would have sounded ungrateful. She was very
grateful; she had only to remember the horrid basement
flat to be awash with gratitude.

Wednesday already, she thought happily as she got her
breakfast the next morning, three more days and she
would be at the lodge again. She washed up, saw to
Nelson, tidied the flat and skipped downstairs and
unlocked the waiting-room door, pulled the curtains
back, opened the windows and went to unlock the
consulting room. The door wasn't locked; after a second
of hesitation, she opened it wide. Professor Culver was at
his desk, writing. He looked up briefly, said irritably,
'Well, don't gape like that—make me some coffee, will
you? I'll be gone in ten minutes or so, but until then I
don't want to be disturbed.'

Meg prudently said nothing but left him there to get
out the percolator and his cup and saucer. He was
wearing a sweater and he needed a shave—she was an
observant girl—he'd been up all night, or at least part of
it, and she could forgive him for being testy.

She went back within a few minutes with the coffee,
hot and milky and sweet, put it on the desk and skimmed
silently to the door.

'Had your breakfast?' enquired the Professor as he
flung down his pen.

'Yes, thank you.' She opened the door wide enough to
go through and was halted by his, 'Get yourself some
coffee and come back here. Please,' he added, in such a
mild voice that she did as she was bid, fetched a mug and
sat down in Miss Standish's chair, the one she used when
she was taking letters. She did it soundlessly and with
composure. If he wanted company he should have it. She
didn't think he would want to chat and she had no
intention of starting a conversation.

He sat back in his chair, the mug in his hand. 'Mrs James and her small daughter Nancy are coming at half past nine. I've given Miss Standish the morning off. Mrs James is young and, for want of a better word, frivolous. Nancy has a sarcoma which I'm almost certain can be cured, but her mother is going to take the news badly. I shall want you to cope with her—you have phlegm and common sense . . .'

Meg took a sip of coffee. Compliments, if one could call them that, were flying. She said quietly, 'Very well, Professor Culver. Would you like some more coffee?'

When she had fetched it he asked, 'Are you happy here, Meg?'

'Yes, thank you.' She finished her own coffee and sat without fidgeting, ready to answer politely if questioned. It was quiet in the room and their silence lasted rather too long. The Professor put down his cup and she heard his sigh.

'Will you tell Nurse that I'll be back at nine-twenty?'

She collected the mugs and went back to the little kitchen, and soon heard him leave. She dearly wanted to know why he had been up during the night. She would find out from Miss Standish after their dinner hour; meanwhile there was nothing to do until Mary Giles arrived.

She received the news of the Professor's disturbed night with a shake of her head. 'He's a consultant, love, and a lecturer too, travels the world . . . and he's an expert if ever there was one, yet if there is a hitch he'll think nothing of spending hours at the hospital. There are Mrs James and Nancy coming too, they were here just before you came and he told her then that there would be tests on the child and it might be necessary for her to have some hospital treatment. She wouldn't listen, of course. The child's as good as gold, but the mother . . .'

Mrs Giles rolled her eyes upwards. 'And Miss Standish at the dentist!'

'Yes, well, the Professor said I was to look after Mrs James.'

'Rather you than me, love!'

The Professor arrived soon afterwards, immaculate in his dark grey suit and Italian silk tie and looking none the worse for his sleepless night. Hard on his heels came Mrs James and Nancy.

Reflecting later upon her morning while she ate her sandwiches and fed Nelson, Meg hoped there would never be another one like it. Nancy had been a model patient, but her mother had at first refused to listen to the Professor, and after a patient ten minutes or so on his part, had declared roundly that no one in her family or her husband's had ever had cancer and she wasn't going to believe him. 'Nancy will be a cripple—you say it's one of her legs.' She burst into angry tears.

The Professor said sternly, 'There is no reason to suppose that radiotherapy will turn Nancy into a cripple, Mrs James.'

It was then that Meg was summoned to bring tea. Which she did, and was told to stay. She poured out for Mrs James, murmured soothingly and melted into a corner. 'I'll simply not believe it,' said Mrs James, and sipped her tea.

The Professor examined his nails. 'It's the child's life, Mrs James. Perhaps I could have a word with your husband?'

Mrs James held her cup out for more tea. 'Well, I suppose you know what you're talking about,' she said rudely. 'You'd better come and see him, I suppose.'

Meg had to admire his bland silkiness. 'Meg, fetch my appointments book, if you will,' and when he had it, 'I can spare fifteen minutes this evening, Mrs James. If your husband would be good enough to come here at half past six? He will be back in London by then?'

He gave Meg the book. 'Tell Nurse that Mrs James is ready to leave, please. She's upstairs with Nancy.'

There had been twenty minutes or so before the next patient; she had taken in his coffee and marvelled at his calm after all that hassle. She and Mrs Giles, snatching a quick cup of tea, agreed that even allowing for overwrought feelings, Mrs James had been awful.

The Professor would be at Maud's all that afternoon and Mrs Giles would go home as soon as she had set the examination room to rights and got things ready for the next day, which gave Meg a chance to take a little time off after her lunch and do some shopping. She came back with a laden basket, saw Mrs Giles away and set about putting the reception room in a state of pristine order. She tidied the consulting room too, being very careful to arrange the muddle on the desk in exactly the way it had been before, and by then it was time to lock up for the evening. She hadn't forgotten that the Professor would be back, but he could let himself in. She took the keys with her and went upstairs.

She had fed Nelson, done a few small chores and was contemplating the contents of the fridge with a view to making supper when the doorbell rang. It would be Percy to collect her rubbish; she opened the door and was met by the Professor's austere, 'Never open the door without first putting up the chain, Meg.'

She opened the door wide and invited him in, prudently forbearing from answering him back. Once inside, he stood in the centre of the room, towering over everything, dwarfing the table and chairs. He had the look of a man who needed soothing, but she wasn't sure how to set about it.

'Will you sit down?'

He ignored that. 'I have the urge to talk,' he said testily, 'and for some reason I find you a good listener.

Come back to my house and have dinner with me, Meg?'

If he had told her to jump off the balcony she couldn't have been more surprised. Surely there were half a dozen girls who would fit the bill far better than she. He saw her hesitation and added blandly, 'Never timid, Meg? I shouldn't have thought it of you.'

'Certainly not,' she said sharply, quite forgetting to be self-effacing. She remembered just in time to add meekly, 'I was a little surprised, Professor.' She looked so demure that he gave her a second glance. 'But of course I'll come.' She made it sound as though he had asked her to run an errand in her free time, and he frowned.

She gave him a kind smile. 'I'll fetch my coat.'

She had changed into a skirt and sweater after work and she was hardly dressed for an evening out, but that couldn't be helped. She put on some more lipstick, ran a comb through her hair and went back to the sitting-room.

The Professor was standing where she had left him, studying Nelson, who was sitting very erect in his box, watching him.

'He looks more like a cat,' commented the Professor laconically. Meg opened her mouth to make the obvious answer to that and then closed it again; she said with her new-found meekness, 'Yes, doesn't he? I'm ready, Professor Culver.'

She switched off all but one table lamp and opened the door, stopping to make sure that she had the key.

The Rolls was at the kerb and she got in without fuss. She had no idea where he lived and she longed to ask, but she wasn't going to. Before her father and mother died they had visited London often enough; he drove towards Regent's Park, past Gloucester Gate and turned in the direction of the Grand Union Canal.

Little Venice, Meg reflected silently; she had a vague recollection of it, tucked away, a much sought-after spot.

The Professor drove past the row of handsome houses overlooking the canal and a hundred yards further on stopped before a brick house standing on its own. It was older than the other dwellings there and while not large, was built in a higgledy-piggledy style which suggested that from time to time its owners had added a room here and there, a hooded iron balcony jutting out over the street and an oriel window and what Meg took to be an Adam doorway.

There was a narrow strip of grass between the house and the pavement and a short flagstone path to the front door. Light streamed from the downstairs windows and from the fanlight over the door, and when the Professor unlocked it, Meg found herself in a square hall lit by a cut-glass chandelier. There were thin silky rugs on the polished wooden floor and a porter's chair in one corner with a marble-topped console table against either wall.

The Professor was behind her, urging her on, and coming towards them from the door beside the gracefully curved staircase was a tall and very stout middle-aged woman, dressed severely in black.

The Professor addressed her in a genial voice. 'Rosie, I've brought Miss Collins from the consulting rooms to keep me company at dinner. Show her where she can leave her coat, will you?' He glanced at Meg. 'Rosie is an old family friend; she housekeeps for me.'

Meg offered a hand and looked up into Rosie's face. Unlike the rest of her appearance, it wasn't severe at all. She found herself smiling at the shrewd blue eyes twinkling at her.

She regretted the plainness of her appearance; in the small, elegant cloakroom she did the best she could with her hair and her face, feeling quite inadequate in such a splendid house. Not that it mattered, she consoled herself; the Professor never looked at her for long enough to know if she was wearing a sack or a ballgown.

He stuck his head round a door as she went back into the hall, and then opened it wide for her to go in. The room was facing the canal, and the long velvet curtains were still undrawn over the wide windows. There was a brisk fire in the grate facing them and a deep couch and chairs arranged around it. Meg took the chair he offered her and glanced around her, trying not to appear too inquisitive. The colours were charming, a mixture of tawny browns and rich cream with a hint of apricot lamps and cushions, mingling nicely with the maple lamp tables and the rosewood rent table by the windows. There was a magnificent walnut and yew wood escritoire against the end wall with spoonbacked buttoned velvet chairs on either side of it, and bowls of spring flowers here and there. A truly lovely room, comfortable to the point of luxury but lived-in too.

She accepted the sherry she was offered and sat quietly, answering her companion's desultory remarks politely without offering any of her own. Presently, across the hall in the dining-room, sitting opposite him at the oval mahogany table, she took care to agree with whatever he said, even though once or twice her wish to argue was very great.

The meal was delicious: artichoke soup, fillets of sole with lobster sauce, a winter salad and to finish, a hot chocolate soufflé served with whipped cream. They went back to the sitting-room for coffee, and not until then did Meg remind him, 'You wanted to talk, Professor . . .'

He was sitting back, his long legs stretched out to the fire, his face in shadow. 'You're a restful companion, Meg; you don't wear jangling bracelets, nor do you whip out a mirror and stare at your face every half-hour or so.'

'I expect if I had bracelets to jangle and a face to admire I'd do that too.'

She couldn't see his smile. 'I was beginning to wonder what had come over you—not a single waspish remark for two days! I feared that you were sickening for something.'

'I had no intention of being waspish.' Her voice achieved meekness once more. 'I'm sorry.'

She sat back in her chair, her hands in her lap, so self-effacing that she might not have been there. Presently she said, 'I'm listening . . .'

He gave a little laugh. 'Determined to sing for your supper, aren't you, Meg? What did you think of little Nancy this morning?'

'A dear little girl—she has no idea that she's ill, I imagine?'

'Perhaps she knows a little—you see, she has pain from time to time—not bad at the moment. Thanks to an observant nanny, we can deal with that and, with God's good grace, cure her. And her mother?'

Meg said carefully, 'It's harder for some people—I mean when they get bad news or things go wrong.'

'I had a talk with Nancy's father.' The Professor suddenly sounded tired. 'Sometimes I almost lose faith in my fellow beings, Meg.'

'Well, you mustn't. Where would we all be without clever men like you?'

He said in a surprised voice, 'You really mean that, don't you?'

'Of course I do!' She had forgotten about being meek. 'You're tired, you need to go to bed early and sleep soundly.' She stirred in her chair. 'I'm going back now so that you can do just that.'

It was silly to feel disappointed when he said quietly, 'Why, that's a good idea, Meg,' for it meant that she had to get to her feet with every appearance of satisfaction; she could have sat there in the peace of the lovely room for hours, just listening. Only he hadn't wanted a listener, just someone to keep him company for an hour while he unwound from a difficult day. She got her coat and

wished Rosie a civil good night, then followed him out to
the door and into the car, sitting quietly beside him as he
drove the short distance back to the consulting rooms. At
the door she undid her seat belt and reached for the
handle, but his hand came down on hers. 'Wait.' So she
waited while he got out and ushered her out and took the
door key from her and, rather to her surprise, went
upstairs with her. He opened the flat door too, and went
in with her without having been invited. Nelson was still
in his box, asleep, and the room was warm and
welcoming in the lamplight. He went to the kitchen and
opened the kitchen door, and glanced along the balcony
before shutting it and locking it again. When he was
standing beside her again, Meg said, 'Thank you for my
dinner, Professor; I do hope you have a good night's
sleep.'

'So do I—I'm taking a very glamorous young lady out
for the evening tomorrow—I shall be needing all my
energy.'

'But you'll enjoy it,' observed Meg in a motherly voice.
Then she asked, 'Is she very pretty?'

'Delightfully so. She collects men in the same way as
you collect down-and-out animals.' He gave her a
mocking smile and she went pink. It had been a mistake
to have spent the evening with him. He hadn't wanted
her company; she had been the first thing at hand to
occupy his mind and take his thoughts from his day's
work. She went to the door. 'Good night, Professor.' Her
voice was quite without expression, and she smiled nicely
as he went through the door.

She was shutting it quickly on his broad back when he
turned suddenly and she had to open it again. He said
slowly, 'I don't know why it should be, but you bring out
the worst in me, Meg. I wonder why?' He bent and kissed
her swiftly on one cheek. 'It's a situation which requires

some thought,' he told her in a silky voice which disturbed her.

It continued disturbing her while she got ready for bed. 'Anyone would think that he'd been drinking,' she told Nelson, 'but we only had sherry and wine at dinner. Perhaps he's so tired he doesn't know what he's saying.'

A silly remark, she had to admit; the Professor was a man who would always know what he was saying.

CHAPTER SIX

THERE was no sign of tiredness or drunkenness in Professor Culver when he arrived in the morning. Indeed, in his sober, superbly cut suit he gave Meg the impression that neither of these conditions would dare to intrude upon him. He gave her a suave good morning as he went into his consulting room, and when she went in with his coffee he was already deep in his post, with the faithful Miss Standish taking notes. Meg was left with the supposition that he had made a subtle joke she hadn't understood. As for kissing her, well, everyone kissed everyone these days. She went back to her desk and assumed the mantle of the perfect receptionist.

She was getting rather good at it. All the same, it was a delight to wake up on Saturday morning with the prospect of the weekend at the lodge. That it was pelting with rain did nothing to dampen her spirits; she rose early, got everything ready and went to her morning's work with a light heart.

It was still raining when they left and the Professor, beyond a few remarks about the weather, had nothing to say. But nothing could dampen her pleasure at the prospect of a weekend at the lodge. She gave a quick sigh of contentment as the Professor swept the car through the gates, which changed to a soundless 'Oh!' as he continued past it. She said nothing, and when he leaned across her and undid the door she got out and stood on the sweep before his house. It was surprisingly close to the lodge, but well screened by trees and shrubs, a fair-sized house with fine pargeting and black and white timber cladding. A small manor house, beautifully

maintained. Its mullioned windows and stout front door
gave it the cosy look of a much smaller place and Meg,
studying it, sighed with unconscious envy. To live in such
a delightful home must be everyone's dear dream . . .

'Come inside,' invited the Professor. 'Nelson will be all
right for a few minutes. I'd like you to meet Mr and Mrs
Trugg, who look after the house . . . In case you should
ever need to come here while I'm not at home,' he added
blandly.

Trugg advanced to meet them as they went inside—a
man of about the Professor's age, already going a little
bald and on the stout side. He greeted his employer with
grave pleasure, acknowledged Meg's smile, and with
dignity took her old Burberry as though it were Russian
sable.

The Professor led the way into a long, low room with
windows at either end and a magnificent strapwork
ceiling, furnished mostly with William and Mary period
pieces, blending nicely with the great wing-back armchairs on either side of the William Cheave fireplace.
The leaded windows were small and curtained with
mulberry satin. Quite perfect, reflected Meg, taking it all
in without saying a word.

'Such a miserable day,' commented her companion.
'Have you had lunch?' He didn't give her a chance to
answer. 'Of course you haven't—there was no time.' He
tugged an old-fashioned bell rope by the fireplace, and
when Trugg came, he asked for coffee and sandwiches.

He was about to sit down when three dogs nosed their
way past Trugg and rushed across the room. The first two
were bull terriers, the third was Lucky. He made for Meg,
greeted her with a good deal of excitement and then went
to the Professor's chair, reared up to look into his face
and then returned to sit by her.

'Ben and Polly,' said the Professor, and at a wave of his
hand they went obediently to her. She patted their heads,

careful to keep a hand on Lucky. 'Don't worry, they get on well,' he said. 'We'll walk them back to the lodge presently and they can meet Nelson—then if he happens to stray this way they won't do anything, if they've made friends.'

The coffee and sandwiches came, and Meg allowed the Professor to make conversation, giving polite answers from time to time but making no effort to attract his attention with any remarks of her own. Soon, when they got up to go, she caught him looking at her with a puzzled frown. Really looking, she was pleased to see, not just a hasty glance. She accepted her old mac from Trugg, waited while the Professor got her bag and Nelson in his box from the car, and walked beside him down the drive and round the curve which hid the house from the lodge. She was a bit apprehensive for Nelson, who was watching the dogs with a watchful eye, but when they got to the lodge, the Professor set the box down in the porch, spoke to his dogs, who merely sniffed at Nelson, and opened the door. He put her bag down on the floor, lifted Nelson's box on to the table, bade her a pleasant goodbye and with the dogs at his heels started back along the drive.

Meg just had time to thank him for her lunch. He nodded vaguely. 'My pleasure—we'll leave tomorrow about six o'clock.'

Meg, trotting round doing her small chores and lighting the fire, wondered if the girl was going to join him again and, without actually being aware of doing so, listened out for his car to pass the lodge. But it didn't; she did her shopping with Lucky, had tea round the fire, found the tapestry work she had taken up when her mother was ill, and spent a blissful evening with no sounds but the radio and Lucky and Nelson's snores.

It was still raining when she got up the next morning. She took Lucky for a walk, got her dinner ready and then went into the garden; there was a lot to do, whatever the weather. She was happily grubbing up weeds on either side of the little gate when two cars went past. The girl was in the first one, sitting beside the driver, and there were people in the back. The second car was full too, and they had hardly disappeared round the curve when Mrs Culver's old-fashioned car appeared. Mrs Culver was sitting in the back and the car slowed and stopped at the gate.

'Ralph said you would be here,' began Mrs Culver. 'How delightful to see you, my dear; aren't you getting rather wet?'

'It's nice to be out of doors, and I quite like the rain. How are you, Mrs Culver?'

'Splendid. I must tell Betsy I've seen you. You're happy, Meg?'

'Very happy, Mrs Culver.'

'You're not coming up to the house for lunch?'

'Oh, my goodness, no!' And then, in case Mrs Culver should be offended, 'There's so much that I want to do here.' She looked down at her small untidy person. 'Besides, I'm hardly dressed for it . . .'

Mrs Culver beamed at her. 'Perhaps not, dear, but you look rather nice all the same—wholesome is the word.' She sat back and Noakes started the car again, and Meg went back to her weeding; she wasn't quite sure if she liked being called wholesome—it sounded like a wholemeal loaf.

She was washing up after her lunch when she heard the cars going past, but she resisted the temptation to peep from the sitting-room window.

It was going to rain all day; she got into the Burberry again, got Lucky's lead and went for another walk. The hedges were drenched, but here and there were primroses tucked away under the trees. She picked a small bunch to take back with her to the flat and went back to make tea, feed the animals and get ready to leave. It was almost six o'clock when the Professor thumped on the door, and when Meg opened it he came in with Ben and Polly, who, obedient to his quiet command, sat down and stared inscrutably at the opposite wall.

His enquiry as to whether she had enjoyed her weekend was perfunctory, but all the same she answered it with enthusiasm, nicely damped down to a wooden politeness.

'Well, it's more than I have.' His eye fell on the primroses, neatly wrapped in damp paper. 'You went walking?'

'Oh, yes. I don't mind the rain. You'd like to take Lucky now?'

She bade the faithful beast goodbye, and the Professor turned on his heel, whistled to his own dogs and strode off.

He came back again presently, loaded Nelson into the car, waited while she locked the door and then shut the car door on her with something of a snap. It seemed prudent to remain silent, and not a word was uttered until they were within five minutes of the consulting rooms.

'In two weeks' time I shall be taking my mother over to Amsterdam. We shall be there a week. Remind me to check the appointments book with you in the morning.'

'Very well, Professor.' Meg had been taken by surprise, but she didn't allow it to show.

He drew up and got out of the car, accompanied her to the flat, waited until she had lighted a table lamp, stalked to the balcony and looked around and then with a brief good night, went away.

'Very upset,' said Meg to Nelson. 'Perhaps he's had a tiff with that girl. A holiday will do him good. Do you suppose we'll be able to spend a week at the lodge or stay here with nothing to do?'

But in fact the week was to be spent quite differently,

as she discovered in the morning.

The morning patients were all for check-ups and the first one wouldn't come until ten o'clock; in the afternoon the Professor would be at the hospital presiding over his outpatients' clinic. Meg, her chores done and the coffee percolating, gave him a cheerful good morning when he arrived, but instead of going into his consulting room he crossed to the desk.

'Those appointments,' he began. 'The check-ups for the week when I shall be away can be fitted in on the week following; there are several new patients—get them on the phone, please, and make appointments for the week before I go. Fit them in where you can; if necessary we can work until six o'clock.'

He sat down on the edge of the desk. 'Now listen to me, Meg. While my mother is away, Kate is to have a holiday, Betsy will stay and Noakes and his wife will move in to keep her company. We shall be staying with my grandmother, whose elderly housekeeper could do with a few days' rest. My mother hopes that you will consider coming with us and acting as housekeeper in her stead.'

Meg didn't say anything for a long moment; such a wealth of delight and excitement had engulfed her that she couldn't have uttered anyway. Outwardly serene, she looked at him, while she pondered the astounding fact that she had fallen in love; this then was what poets since the world began had been writing about, this delightful bubbly feeling which made her want to sing and shout, this wild desire to fling herself into the Professor's arms. The remnant of good sense left in her neat head reminded her that he was hardly likely to welcome that; a more unsuitable man with whom to fall in love was surely not to be found.

She said in a quiet voice which gave none of her feelings away, 'I can't speak or understand Dutch. And what about Nelson?' Then after a pause for thought, 'I have no passport.' He was watching her closely.

'My grandmother's household is bilingual. Nelson can go to Much Hadham; he'll be quite safe there. You can get a visitor's passport at the nearest Post Office.' He smiled at her and her heart turned over. 'Just for a week, Meg?'

He could have asked for a lifetime. 'Very well, Professor Culver.'

He got off the desk. 'My mother will be deeply grateful,' he told her. An answer which gave her no satisfaction at all. She watched him leave the room, aware that life would never be the same again and perhaps would not be very happy either.

The week passed: Meg found herself living for the moment when the Professor arrived in the mornings, and that was something which would have to stop, she told herself repeatedly. As soon as she could, she would look for another job where she wouldn't see him and in time, would forget him. This, she had to admit to herself, was wishful thinking; the tiresome man had taken root in her heart and head. She busied herself with plans for her week in Amsterdam; the housekeeper's grey dress, of course, but she had a little money to spend now, a new coat and perhaps a knitted dress to go under it. A pair of boots would also be nice.

Towards the end of the week the Professor went to Birmingham for an afternoon, lecturing, and Meg, offered a couple of hours off after her lunch, took herself out to do some shopping.

She found a tweed coat, beautifully cut, at Jaeger's, and since there was a matching skirt she bought that too, as well as a couple of sweaters to go with it. She had already spent all the money she had planned to, but she was feeling reckless; she hadn't needed much of the money she had earned and there was her share of the house in the bank. She made a beeline for Harrods and bought a knitted dress in a pleasing shade of amber and a silk jersey two-piece in several shades of old rose. She thought it unlikely that she would wear it, but she would feel happier if she had something pretty with her. One never knew ... She left the thought hanging in the air and wandered into the shoe department.

She had intended buying boots and she did, but she bought a pair of high-heeled pumps too and, since she still had time to spare, she stocked up on undies and on more make-up. Then, to round off her afternoon, she had a taxi home.

She had phoned Cora the day before and told her about her week in Amsterdam. Cora had observed that it sounded very nice and added crossly that she couldn't think what had got into Meg, adding that both boys had the measles. She sounded as though it was Meg's fault.

She would have to let Doreen know, but before she had a chance to phone after she got back to the flat, her sister rang.

'What's all this about you going to Amsterdam? As a housekeeper, too—aren't you satisfactory at the consulting rooms? Have you got the sack already?'

Then, before Meg could get a word in edgeways, 'This really won't do, you know, Meg. I blame myself for not insisting on you buying that flat and training as a shorthand typist. You would have got a good steady job in another month or two; now here you are, not trained for anything and heaven knows where you'll end up. That's what comes of letting you have your own way!'

'But I've got a good steady job. I'm perfectly satisfactory; I'm going to Amsterdam to help out Mrs Culver's mother so that her own housekeeper can have a rest—the one who had her feet done, you know. I'm looking forward to it. I can't think why you and Cora are making such a fuss. I'm very happy and I really like the job.'

'Is Professor Culver going?'

'I believe so. Have you settled into your flat?'

'Just about. I'm going to give a housewarming party. You must come and bring Professor Culver—after all, we have met.'

'You can always invite him. Miss Standish, his secretary, says that he has a very busy life.'

'Well, I dare say he might not come unless I asked him myself—you don't hit it off together, do you? I shall ring him up.'

There was one thing about Doreen, Meg reflected as she hung up—she had plenty of self-confidence. She thought it doubtful that the Professor would go. He had his own friends, and by the look of things, the girl she had seen him with most likely occupied most of his leisure. The thought hurt, but stronger than the hurt was the conviction that given the chance she could make the Professor happy. True, he was dictatorial at times and positively testy if he was tired, but if he had a loving wife to go home to, that could be changed. She had little hope of him falling in love with her, but there was no harm in trying . . .

She crossed the room and studied her face in the mirror above the fireplace. It gave her little encouragement; she had experimented with a more elaborate make-up and then discarded it. Hers wasn't that kind of face. Her eyes were all right, she supposed, and the lashes curled long and thick, but not everyone admired grey eyes and her hair, long and fine and silky, was a pale brown which a more enterprising girl would have tinted years ago. She reminded herself that beauty was only skin deep and went to cook her supper. She gave the matter some thought during the evening; there wasn't much she could do except keep a curb on her tongue and present him

with a picture of serenity and meekness. The meekness
would come hard, but she noticed that it puzzled him; at
least it had made him aware of her.

She saw the Professor only briefly on the following
day, and on the Saturday, contrary to his usual practice,
he had several patients. Two of them had come for a first
consultation and took up a great deal of the morning; he
was unhurried in his work, deeming, quite rightly, that
anyone threatened with a possibility of serious illness
had the right to talk about it from every angle. Meg made
appointments for them, made tea for them both and said
all the right things; now she knew a little about the
Professor's work she found it easier to talk to them. With
very few exceptions they reacted well to the Professor's
pleasant, reassuring manner. They drank their tea,
convinced that he would cure them, and since Meg lent a
kindly ear, they discussed their treatment, their domestic
worries and occasionally their fears.

Tidying the waiting-room when the last patient had
gone, Meg reflected that there was nothing sad about her
work; it was like fighting an enemy and mostly winning.
She supposed the Professor felt like that too.

She was just finished when he came into the room.
Miss Standish had gone and she could hear Percy in the
yard clashing the dustbin lids.

'We're late,' observed the Professor, stating the
obvious. 'I'll be back for you in half an hour. Can you get
yourself a sandwich by then and be ready to leave? I've
guests coming for the weekend and I want to get home
before they arrive.'

He barely waited for her answer; she heard the car
leave as she skipped up to the flat, drank some milk, fed
Nelson, gobbled a slice of bread and butter and tore out
of her dress and into a tweed skirt and pullover. She flung
on her Burberry and, snatching up her bag and Nelson's

box, got to the front door just as the Rolls slid to a silent halt before it.

'You had your lunch?' enquired the Professor, stuffing Nelson and her bag on to the back seat.

'Yes, thank you.' Her quiet voice implied contentment, while her hungry insides started to rumble. Their ideas of lunch would hardly be the same. She sat beside him, planning supper to make up for it: steak and tomatoes and courgettes and creamed potatoes, and, since she would have all the time in the world to cook that evening, an egg custard with cream and coffee afterwards.

'You're very quiet,' observed her companion, and then before she could reply, 'you smell like a country garden.'

So the wildly expensive bottle of Anaïs-Anaïs she had bought at Harrods had paid dividends! She thought it prudent to ignore the second part of his remark. 'I'm planning my weekend,' she told him pleasantly.

'What are your plans?' He sounded very faintly bored.

'Walking with Lucky, gardening, shopping.'

He said silkily, 'Sometimes you sound too good to be true, Meg.'

She bit back the retort she had on her tongue. If she said anything else she would sound like a prig. 'The country is beginning to look delightful,' she observed gently.

He mumbled something and drove fast and in silence until they were going through Much Hadham. 'I'll send Lucky down with Trugg.' He stopped the car by the lodge, unloaded Nelson and put her bag in the porch before getting back into the car. 'Enjoy your weekend, such as it is,' he told her. There was mockery in his smile.

The little cottage welcomed her; she saw to Nelson and then, since the shops would close at four o'clock, she put Lucky, handed over by a friendly Trugg, on his lead and walked into Much Hadham. The high street was full of late shoppers, and she enjoyed pottering in and out of the butcher's and the greengrocer's. She bought doughnuts for tea and decided to bake her own bread.

The days were lengthening, but she lit the fire and turned on the lamps when she got back. She had bought a paper and now she sat, eating her doughnuts and drinking cup after cup of tea, the curtains drawn against the dusk, listening to Radio Three. She wasn't happy— she wasn't sure if she would ever be quite happy again— but for the moment she was content.

It was a couple of hours later that she heard voices and the creak of the gate. She was in the kitchen; the steak was under the grill, smelling delicious, the vegetables were on the stove and she was taking two loaves from the oven. When there was a knock on the door she laid them carefully on the kitchen table and went to open it.

The girl was outside, with a tall young man, his face hidden behind a beard and a moustache.

They walked past Meg into the sitting-room and the girl said, 'Hello—we wanted Ralph to bring us but he wouldn't, said you needed privacy or some such nonsense.' She gave a little fluting laugh. 'We escaped while he took those dogs of his for a walk.'

Meg stood in the centre of the little room and looked at them. The girl was every bit as pretty as she had thought, and dressed in the height of fashion, her hair pulled off her face and wound into a strange lop-sided topknot. The man she dismissed as someone she didn't like on sight.

She said politely, 'Good evening,' and then, 'why did you come?'

'We thought we'd do a bit of slumming, my dear.' The girl smiled widely, showing beautiful teeth.

Capped, thought Meg waspishly, and out loud said, 'I'm cooking—you will have to excuse me for a moment . . .'

'My God, can you cook too?' The girl added

deliberately, 'Ralph said you were a pre-war paragon with no ambition. Domesticated too . . .'

She looked round her. 'We'll sit down while you slave over your hot stove.' She took one of the armchairs and raised her eyebrows at Lucky and Nelson, sitting, very much on guard, before the fire. 'I don't think much of your taste in pets,' she said, and laughed at the young man.

None of them heard the Professor coming through the open gate. Ben and Polly nosed their way in the door which had been left ajar, with their master on their heels. He said without preamble, 'I'm so sorry about this, Meg; I must apologise for my guests, they must have misunderstood me. I know you cherish your privacy.' He stared blandly round. 'We'll go at once.'

He opened the door wide and stood by it as the girl swept past him and the young man followed.

'You've been making bread,' declared the Professor as he followed them. 'And I smell something delicious—steak?'

Meg nodded. She was too near tears of rage to speak, and to her shame, two of them trickled down her cheeks before she could swallow them back.

The Professor watched them with an expressionless face. 'Don't worry, this won't happen again,' he told her, and took a step back into the cottage and kissed her gently.

He shut the door quietly behind him and she turned the key, not caring if he heard or not. But she wasn't going to let it spoil her weekend; she finished cooking her supper, fed the animals, laid the plates and glasses and silver she had brought with her from her old home, and turned up the radio. Crying wouldn't help—she knew that; she was more determined than ever that the Professor shouldn't marry that truly awful girl.

Sunday passed twice as fast as any other day in the

week. The morning was fine and cold and she and Lucky walked their fill before going back to the casserole she had put in the oven. There wasn't much of the afternoon left by the time she had washed the dishes and tidied up. The garden was repaying her labours; there were daffodils in bud and grape hyacinths already out as well as the primroses and violets under the hedges. She grubbed round happily and presently went to put the kettle on for tea, thus missing the car, with the bearded man at the wheel, speeding past.

The Professor came to fetch Lucky while she was on her knees emptying ashes from the grate. He frowned when he saw her and asked, 'Do you have to do that?'

Meg thought of several pert answers and said matter-of-factly 'Well, yes, I do.' She got up and fetched Lucky's lead. She bent to fondle him and said briskly, 'Off you go, see you next week. Be a good fellow.'

She assured the Professor with equal briskness that she would be ready when he came, and got down on her knees once again. She had managed to say almost nothing to him, and she had barely glanced at him. She supposed it was because she loved him so much that she could forgive him calling her a domesticated pre-war paragon with no ambition; all the same, it rankled.

The cottage was locked up and she was standing by the gate with Nelson beside her in his box when the Professor came. He said sharply, 'There's no need for you to stand around as though you were waiting for a bus. Stay indoors in future.'

Her 'Very well, Professor,' was uttered in a soothing voice, and he added testily, 'And don't be so damned meek about it!'

They were half-way back to London when he said, 'About next week; we shall leave on Sunday evening. I'll take you down to the lodge as usual on Saturday, and Nelson can go from there to the house. We'll leave in the afternoon and pick up my mother on the way. We shall be going by sea; she doesn't care for flying. Have you got your passport? Good, pack at the flat then, and bring your things with you.'

Meg just stopped herself in time from saying, 'Very well, Professor.'

It was a good thing that she had already done her shopping, for there was no time during the week; the appointments book was full and the Professor worked until six o'clock each evening. What was more, he went to Maud's earlier each morning, so that Meg had to be ready for him well before nine o'clock. In a way she was glad, for it meant that she had little time to reflect on her own problems. She washed and ironed and packed a case and an overnight bag, did her hair and her nails and phoned her sisters, and all the while she was aware of steadily mounting excitement. She would be busy enough in Amsterdam, she supposed, cooking the kind of meals Mrs Culver, and presumably her mother and son, expected would occupy her time and there would be household chores. All the same she would be in the same house as he; it was the last thing she thought of before she went to sleep each night.

Saturday came and it was almost one o'clock when the last patient went away. Meg started to clear up, thinking of all the little jobs she still had to do before she would be finished. Any moment now the Professor would put his head round the door and tell her to be ready in some impossibly short time.

Sure enough, she was putting the final touches to her desk when he appeared. 'I'll be back in half an hour. Be ready with Nelson and your case and don't bother about lunch. We'll have a quick snack at my place.'

She said, 'Very well, Professor,' before she could stop herself, and added a brisk, 'I'll be quite ready.'

It was chilling to be told that she had better be because

he had no intention of waiting for her.

She longed to tell him that he was the rudest man she had ever met, but that would spoil her image.

She had prudently left everything ready in the flat. With five minutes in hand she went down to the hall, wearing the new coat, her overnight bag slung over one shoulder, Nelson, nicely full with his dinner, already snoozing in his box. She had already told Percy that she would be away, and he shouted up a cheerful goodbye from his semi-basement. The house would be quiet with none of them there. Meg sat down on the stairs to wait and took a last look in her handbag to make sure that she had her passport as well as her money. When the street door opened she was sitting, the picture of serenity, one hand on Nelson's battered head. The Professor paused in the doorway to look at her. 'Did I ever tell you that you're too good to be true?' he wanted to know.

'Oh, yes.' She got to her feet and picked up the box, giving him a gentle smile, noting at the same time that he had changed from his sober grey suit to well-worn, beautifully cut tweeds. They made him look approachable and much younger. Her smile widened and, surprisingly he smiled back, but all he said, puzzling her, was, 'Granny will like you.'

Rosie was waiting for them with soup and omelettes and hot coffee, and they made short work of their meal, with just enough conversation to ensure politeness. Meg would have liked to have lingered a while, but her host made it plain that there was to be no hanging around. They were away again in half an hour or so, travelling fast. Perhaps the girl was going to be at Much Hadham; perhaps, heaven forbid, she was going with them to Holland. Meg hadn't thought of that, and it quite spoilt the drive.

At the lodge the Professor offloaded Nelson and her case, unlocked the door and ushered her inside. 'You've had a busy week,' he said surprising her, 'and doubtless you'll have an even busier one after tomorrow. Don't go for a ten-mile walk or dig the garden.' He was at the door. 'I'll be along tomorrow afternoon for Lucky—you'd better come up to the house then with Nelson, otherwise he might feel abandoned. Trugg will be down with Lucky in a few minutes.'

He had gone before she could answer him.

She settled Nelson, got her shopping basket, and when Trugg arrived with the devoted Lucky, she lost no time in going in to Much Hadham to buy food for the three of them. It was a dry, fine afternoon and she enjoyed the walk there and back again with the dog prancing along beside her. Back indoors, she lit the fire and made tea, all the time listening for a car to go past. There was nothing, however, and on Sunday the quiet morning was undisturbed. She pottered in the garden, with an apron over the new skirt and sweater, had an early lunch and settled down to wait for the Professor. He came earlier than she had expected, whistled to Lucky who had rushed off with Ben and Polly and strolled back to the house with Nelson's box under one arm, talking pleasantly about this and that as they went. At the house Trugg was waiting and led the way across the hall and through the door at one side of the wide staircase. The kitchen was beyond, a large, old-fashioned-seeming room, yet fitted out with every modern convenience. The floor was of flagstones with a rug before the Aga. There was an old-fashioned dresser too, with rows of dishes and plates and a vast scrubbed wooden table with a Windsor chair at each end. The sort of kitchen where one could feel at home, decided Meg, and smiled at Mrs Trugg, who beamed back at her.

'So here's the little old cat, miss. I'll take good care of him, don't you worry. He can sit here right by the stove;

the dogs won't touch him. and I'll see he doesn't stray far.'

Meg set the box down by the Aga and Nelson, sensing comfort and cosseting, purred throatily, curled up and closed his eye. 'I know you'll look after him,' she said a little anxiously, 'he's old and not awfully tough . . .'

Mrs Trugg said comfortably, 'He'll stay by the fire, miss, and we'll feed him up—don't you go worrying about him.'

Meg gave him a final pat and followed the Professor out to the car. Questions jostled around inside her head but she wasn't going to ask them. Presumably they would fetch Mrs Culver, then drive to the ferry. Which ferry? she wondered, and occupied the short drive to Hertingfordbury trying to guess.

It was lovely to see Betsy again; Meg, slipping back into her role of housekeeper, helped take in the tea because Kate had already gone for a few days to her niece. Betsy was happy to be on her own, although Noakes and his wife would sleep in the house. 'I'll 'ave the day to meself,' she explained happily to Meg as they got the tea-tray ready. 'I'll have a fair treat. Not that me and Kate don't get on—we do, like an 'ouse on fire.' She eyed Meg lovingly. 'You look smart, Miss Meg. You're happy, aren't you?' She busied herself making the tea. 'That Professor's a nice man to work for, no doubt.'

'Very nice, Betsy, and I'm very happy.'

They left soon after they had had tea, with Mrs Culver in the back of the car. 'So that I can doze if I want to,' she observed. 'It's so very nice to see you again, Meg, and such a relief that you're coming with us. I'm sure you'll enjoy being in Amsterdam—there's a lot to see.'

Meg agreed politely and wondered if she would have a chance to see anything of the city. She rather doubted it. Just for the moment she was happy, true; the Professor had very little to say for himself, but just to sit beside him was a secret delight. She still didn't know which ferry they would travel on, but when he reached Bishop's Stortford and took the Braintree road she guessed that it would be Harwich.

She settled back in her seat, her head turned a little sideways so that she could watch the Professor's handsome profile. For the moment she was content. The week ahead of her held she knew not what, but some of it must be good; her clothes were right, she had done her best with her hair and face and there was no sign of that girl. She sank into a kind of euphoria until the Professor's voice smoothly dispersed it.

'My grandmother is old, Meg. Eighty-four next birthday. She has a sharp tongue and there's nothing wrong with her intellect. She's also very outspoken. I hope you'll remember that and not let her upset you. She speaks English—she lived here most of her married life—her housekeeper is English, too—elderly; she could do with a few days' rest. There's a maid who lives in and a daily woman; all you'll need to do is to arrange the meals and cook and see that the house is run smoothly.'

He paused, waiting, no doubt, for Meg to make some tart rejoinder. She said merely, 'I shall do my best, Professor.' And listened to his sigh.

He drove in silence for some miles. From where she was sitting he looked cross, and without stopping to mind her tongue she said, 'You're annoyed—why?'

He shot her a sharp glance. 'Not annoyed—puzzled, Meg. You've changed—and don't ask me how because I don't know ... You're hiding; the real you is tucked away out of reach.'

So he had noticed her, enough to remark upon it. A small triumph which warmed her. 'I'm just the same,' she pointed out quietly.

He frowned. 'When you're here I don't notice you, but when you're not I find myself wondering where you are and what you're doing.'

She tried to think of an answer to that and couldn't. Luckily Mrs Culver asked something or other of her son and he said nothing more. A good thing, because Meg had plenty to think about.

CHAPTER SEVEN

At Harwich they embarked with little delay and were taken to their cabins. Meg was standing in the middle of hers, contemplating its comfort, when the stewardess came back with a message. She was to go to the bar by the restaurant as soon as she was ready. So she tidied her hair and did things to her face and found her way to the bar where Mrs Culver and her son were already sitting. They talked over their sherry, mostly of Holland and Amsterdam in particular; presently they had dinner, and then, when they had had their coffee, Meg excused herself and went to her cabin. They would dock quite early in the morning and she would be called with tea and toast, the Professor had told her; he made no effort to detain her.

She slept soundly and was up on deck in time to watch the ferry nose its way into the quay. There was no sign of either Mrs Culver or the Professor when a voice requested passengers to rejoin their cars. Meg went back to her cabin, picked up her overnight bag and made her way down to the car deck. She met the Professor on the way, coming to look for her. He said tersely, 'I've been all over the boat looking for you . . .'

'Good morning, Professor Culver.' She sounded tolerant of someone who wasn't in the best of tempers. 'I was on deck watching us dock. It was most interesting.'

To which he answered with a grunt.

Mrs Culver was already in the car, placidly waiting for whatever came next. She had slept well, she assured Meg, and wasn't it pleasant to be in Holland again? 'Such an easy journey,' she observed, 'since Ralph sees to everything.'

She settled herself more comfortably. 'Are you hungry, dear? It's about ninety kilometres to Amsterdam—only a little over an hour's driving, but I dare say Ralph will stop for coffee on the way.'

Which Meg knew from experience was that lady's way of making sure that they did.

They drove to Den Haag, the traffic already thick although it was still early enough, but the Professor wove his way through the city and on to the motorway to Amsterdam and presently pulled in at a roadside café. It was a cheerful spot, with rows of flags flying before it, and all its lights on. A great improvement on the service stations in England, Meg considered, following Mrs Culver into a room furnished with little tables and chairs surrounding a billiard table. There were several people there, drinking coffee, playing the fruit machines and talking among themselves. They exchanged good mornings and sat down at a table by the window. The coffee was rich and creamy, served in small cups, and they drank it slowly while Mrs Culver talked, her lively chatter covering her companion's silence.

They went on their way again, with the Professor pointing out the various towns they were bypassing. As they circumnavigated Schiphol he said, 'We shall be in the outskirts of Amsterdam in a few minutes. My grandmother lives in the heart of the city, just off the Herengracht.'

Meg had no idea where or what that was; she murmured and looked out of the window at the blocks of modern flats on either side. Very disappointing; she had expected old gabled houses and canals.

Both of which she very soon got. Without hesitation the Professor left the main road and drove in and out of narrow streets bisected by enough canals to satisfy the most demanding of sightseers. He stopped finally half-way down a cul-de-sac facing a canal and lined with the tall, gabled houses which Meg had expected to see. The houses, alike in age, were all different. Each had its own type of gable, and one or two had steep tiled roofs without gables. They leaned against each other, their massive doors firmly shut against the world outside, their large windows gleaming with highly polished glass. The Professor got out, helped his mother and turned to Meg. She was already on the narrow cobbled pavement, her eyes everywhere, trying to see everything at once.

Mrs Culver skipped up the worn stone steps before the door and tugged the old-fashioned bell. The door opened, although Meg couldn't see anyone there, and they went inside. The hall was long and narrow with an elaborate plaster ceiling and tiled floor. There was a staircase at the end, but half-way along the hall there was a lift, tucked away in the panelled wall. It took them to the second floor and opened on to another narrow hallway with a large mahogany door in its centre. That opened as they got out of the lift and a tall, bony woman advanced to welcome them. She was elderly with grey hair and bright blue eyes; she greeted Mrs Culver warmly and then turned to the Professor. 'Well, Ralph, it's a while since you were here; your grandmother will be so pleased . . .' She glanced at Meg and smiled. 'And you'll be the young lady who's to take my place, and indeed I'm grateful for a few days.'

She stood aside and they went into a wide lobby with a number of doors in it. Mrs Culver went straight to the double doors facing them and flung them open, breaking into a flood of Dutch as she did so.

'Come and meet my grandmother,' invited the Professor. He flung an arm around the housekeeper. 'You don't change, Nanny. It's good to see you again. I'll bring Meg to you as soon as she has met Grandmother.'

He gave Meg a prod between the shoulders and she went ahead of him into the room. It was high ceilinged and the walls were panelled. There was a good deal of dark, heavy furniture, all very old and beautifully polished, and an elaborate cast-iron stove with a great mantelshelf above it.

The dusting, thought Meg, making her way towards the old lady sitting in a high-backed chair near the window. There were china ornaments everywhere too and cabinets of silver against the walls. She came to a halt and stood quietly while the old lady inspected her.

'Small, but neat.' The voice was clear and surprisingly youthful. 'Nice face, too. I hope you will be happy here, my dear; I'm very glad to welcome you.'

Meg murmured suitably and wondered what to do next. The Professor came to her rescue. 'When we've had coffee I'll hand Meg over to Florence so that she can get her bearings.' He bent to kiss the old lady. 'As pretty as ever, I see, Granny.'

She chuckled. 'Save your pretty speeches for all the pretty girls you know,' she told him. 'Here's the coffee.'

Presently the Professor took Meg across the lobby and into the kitchen where Florence was waiting. There was a young woman there too, cleaning vegetables at the sink. 'Anna,' he explained, 'the housemaid. She doesn't speak English but that won't matter—she knows her work.'

He went away and Florence said kindly, 'A bit of an upheaval for you, miss, but Anna here is a good girl and there's Mevrouw Til who comes in to do the rough. Come and see your room. Anna's brought the bags up so you can unpack later on.'

The flat was a good deal larger than Meg had thought. Her room was at the end of a narrow passage and down three steps. At the back of the house, it overlooked a very narrow long garden and was most comfortably furnished. 'There's a shower room through that door,' Florence pointed out. 'Anna will sleep across the passage and call you each morning. We could sit down for a moment while I tell you how the place is run.'

Not so different from her own home, Meg decided. Meal times were earlier, and there would be very little cooking required until dinner in the evening. Shopping would be no difficulty: Florence would leave a list of the various things to buy, and besides, she had stocked up with as much as possible. 'Meat and fish mostly,' she said comfortably, 'and you can point out what you want. Do you understand the money?' Going over the various coins didn't take long, and the bank notes were straightforward. 'Now, as to the work around the flat . . .'

That didn't take long to explain either; what did take time were the small likes and dislikes of Professor Culver's grandmother. 'Not very active, but eyes like a hawk,' declared Florence. 'Enjoys her food and everything has to be just so. I'll show you the table silver and linen cupboard.'

Meg didn't go back to the drawing-room, but helped set the table in the sombre dining-room and went to the kitchen to watch the lunch being prepared. A variety of breads, cheeses and cold meats, a salad and omelettes to cook at the last minute. She was breaking eggs into a bowl when she was summoned to the drawing-room.

'You will have your meals with us, naturally,' said the old lady. 'Tell Nanny to set another place if she hasn't already done so.'

'Well, I set the table for three, and if you don't mind, I'd rather have my meals in the kitchen.'

'I do mind. You'll kindly do what I ask without arguing. When you have seen to the table, come back here—for a glass of sherry.'

Meg said, 'Very well,' and saw that the Professor was smiling. She gave him a cold look as she went out of the room. It was obvious that he had inherited a good slice of his grandmother's character as well as her black eyes.

It was a good thing that she had bought the pink dress; it couldn't compete with the old lady's black, high-necked, long-sleeved velvet, or with her daughter's blue crêpe, but at least it provided a suitable background. Both ladies were wearing pearls and several beautiful rings, and the elder also wore a tortoiseshell lorgnette on a gold chain through which she studied Meg at some length. The Professor studied Meg too, but with more discretion.

Florence went after breakfast the next day and Meg, neat and businesslike in her sober grey dress, set about her duties. The Professor had driven Florence to the station and hadn't returned, and it wasn't until she had taken the coffee tray into the drawing-room that she learned that he wouldn't be back until the evening.

'This is supposed to be a break for him,' explained his mother, 'but I doubt if he has much free time. He'll be in Leiden all day, and tomorrow he's lecturing at one of the hospitals and I know he has at least two consultations. Of course he'll have his evenings, but he has friends here; he'll be out again after dinner or will be dining out.'

Meg went back to the kitchen, poured coffee for herself and Anna and sat down to drink it. The week she had been looking forward to didn't promise much after all. She had hoped that she would see something of the Professor at meals; he might have offered to show her something of Amsterdam, but she could see now that her modest expectations had left her in a fool's paradise. She finished her coffee, got the list Florence had given her, made sure that the two ladies were happily gossiping in the drawing-room, and took herself out to the shops.

They were ten minutes' walk away, and Florence had thoughtfully drawn a little street map for her. When she reached them, the shops were very like those at home. She enjoyed the little outing; no one seemed to mind that she couldn't speak Dutch, and indeed quite a few of the

shop assistants spoke English. In a day or two, when she
had some idea of the day's pattern, she would go and see
the sights.

She certainly had no time to go sight-seeing on that
first day; true, of course, Mrs Culver and her mother
both took a nap after their lunch, but Meg, anxious to
appear at her best, spent the afternoon in the kitchen
preparing dinner, and by the time she had done that it
was time to take in the tea-tray.

She wore the pink dress again that evening, and
blushed faintly at the Professor's thoughtful stare. Well,
he would see it each evening whether he liked it or not.
She lifted her firm little chin, wished him a cool good
evening and went to the kitchen to don an apron and dish
up.

She had been quick to hear that when she wasn't with
them, they all three spoke Dutch; once dinner was over
and she brought in the coffee she excused herself and
slipped out of the room. Anna had the evening off; the
dining-room would have to be cleared and breakfast set
for the morning. Meg trotted to and fro, making almost
no noise, and finally shut the kitchen door, put on her
apron once more and started the washing up. It was a
double sink and there was a splendid plate rack above it.
She decided to do the silver separately, and with the
plates and dishes drying themselves, set to work on the
silver, worn thin with age, and she guessed valuable.

She was polishing the spoons when the Professor said
from the door, 'Oh, dear, oh, dear, Granny wants to
know where you are. Why are you washing up?'

She swallowed a waspish reply. 'Anna has the evening
off . . .'

'Well, leave it for her in the morning.'

She forgot about being unobtrusive and meek. 'Don't
be silly; she has enough to do in the mornings and you

want your breakfast at eight o'clock sharp and I'll be busy with the trays.'

He said softly, 'Perhaps this wasn't such a good idea after all . . .'

'It will be perfectly all right provided everyone remembers that I'm the housekeeper.'

He took the teacloth from her and embarked upon the forks. 'I for one,' he observed in his blandest voice, 'never think of you as that. I believe that my mother and Granny live in a world where the washing up does itself and food cooks itself too. They're rather too old to change their views, but I'll see what I can do to lighten your burden.'

Meg rounded on him. 'You'll do no such thing! I came here to housekeep and that's what I'm going to do.'

'Ah, that's more like you, Meg!'

She instantly assumed her mantle of meekness. 'It's very kind of you to offer to help, but it's quite unnecessary, Professor Culver.'

He went on drying the silver. 'What free time do you have, Meg?' He sounded casually friendly.

'Oh, I'm sure I shall get an hour or so in the afternoons.'

'Good, I'll take you to the Rijksmuseum and the Dam Palace—oh, and Rembrandt's museum, and of course, there's the canal trip—you mustn't miss that.'

He put down the last of the forks and, throwing down the cloth, sat on the edge of the table.

She started putting the silver in the baize-lined box. 'Well, that's very kind of you, but I couldn't spare the time for all that; there's dinner to prepare and cook.'

'There are four afternoons before we return. Each day we will try to visit one of the places I've told you about. Better still, one evening Anna can do the washing up and whatever else you do after dinner, and we'll stroll round the town.'

He got off the table. 'Now dry your hands and take off that apron and come and make a fourth at bridge. I warn you that both my mother and Granny cheat if they can!'

Meg was up early the next morning, cooking bacon, eggs, fried bread and mushrooms for the Professor's breakfast. Beyond wishing him good morning, she said nothing, and she doubted if he was aware of who it was serving his breakfast. She went back to the kitchen and started to get the breakfast trays ready; once the Professor was out of the house, she and Anna would have their own meal and then get on with the chores. She heard the front door shut with a heavy thump and she whisked back to the dining-room with a tray, intent on clearing the table. The Professor was standing by the window, gazing idly at the street below.

'Oh, I heard the front door—I thought you'd gone! I'll come back,' she said hastily.

'Can't get rid of me fast enough, Meg? Don't worry, I'll not be back until this evening, I'm going to Groningen.'

Her heart sank; she was seeing even less of him than she did at home. 'I hope you have a pleasant day,' she told him. 'It must make a nice change for you . . .'

His smile mocked her. 'To lecture medical students in Dutch, exchange views with my colleagues at various hospitals, make small talk over drinks with pretty girls— I do all that in England, Meg—my idea of a nice change is hardly the same as yours!' He turned round to face her. 'Now that, for me, would be a quiet afternoon wandering round Amsterdam, showing you the sights. It's time you had a few hours to yourself. We'll do that tomorrow, after lunch. I'm sure you're quite capable of planning a meal which doesn't need your presence in the kitchen for the entire day.'

He strolled to the door. 'Will you spend the afternoon with me, Meg?'

Her heart leapt. 'If it can be arranged and Mrs Culver

bells, and then into Kalverstraat. There were shops here, but he didn't linger, turning off instead into a peaceful little square with a church in its centre and ringed by quaint old almshouses. 'The Begijnsteeg,' he told her, and here he allowed her to linger and peer inside the church. 'Given to the English Reformed Church three hundred years ago,' he told her, and waited patiently while she wandered around.

She went reluctantly, wanting to stay in the quiet place—it would have been nice to sit down with him and talk, but when he took her arm and asked, 'What about tea? There's a good place close by,' she agreed readily, worried that he might be getting impatient with what to him must be a dull afternoon.

He took her to the Sonesta Hotel and gave her a splendid tea, the waitress offering her a great tray of rich cream cakes which she eyed with a childish pleasure which her companion, did she but know it, found vaguely pathetic. He remembered the spoilt girl he had spent the previous evening with, how she had demanded champagne and caviare and fresh peaches and accepted them as her right, and here was Meg getting the maximum enjoyment out of cream cakes. He studied her face and noticed—not for the first time—the dark curling lashes resting on her healthy pink cheeks. He found that he had got into the habit of watching her when he was with her—because she was restful, he supposed, and didn't chatter all the time. Indeed, once or twice he wished she had more to say for herself. She had changed in the past few weeks, become quiet and meek, as though she didn't want him to notice her . . .

'We'll stroll as far as the Dam Palace,' he told her as they left the hotel, 'so that you can see the square and the War Memorial. We can take a taxi back from there. You're not tired?'

Meg turned a glowing face to him. 'Oh, no—it's been

lovely. I've seen such a lot; you've been very kind.'

There was a great street organ playing by the palace; she stood listening to it until she caught sight of her companion's face. Bland indifference, she thought—I must be as tiresome to him as a child being taken to see the sights. She said, 'I'm sorry—you must find all this so tedious.'

He gave her a keen glance; she meant it, too. He signalled a taxi and carried on an undemanding conversation until they arrived back at the flat.

She thanked him again in the hall and saw the small frown of annoyance, although he replied civilly enough as he opened the drawing-room door for her.

She didn't stay long, only to say that she was back and to ask if either lady wanted anything before she started on the dinner. Within ten minutes, once more in her grey dress, she was in the kitchen, tying an apron round herself, putting the soup to warm, beating eggs for the jam soufflé, collecting things for a winter salad, and getting the salmon she had poached the day before while Anna finished setting the table.

Presently, when she had everything organised, she went back to her room and got into the pink dress once more. Mrs Culver's mother, with sublime indifference to the amount of work to be done in the kitchen, expected her to sit in the drawing-room and drink her sherry each evening.

The Professor wasn't at dinner. His grandmother, pecking daintily at the salmon, observed that she had seen very little of him. 'But I suppose he needs his pleasure—he works hard enough and she's a pretty girl.' She looked at her daughter. 'Do you suppose he's serious this time?'

Mrs Culver shook her head and gave a small, secret smile. 'No, not this time. I know he wanted to see Professor Tacx again—after all, he studied under him for several years—and I dare say he wants to see if Julie has grown into a pretty woman—she's been in America, you know.'

With which unsettling conversation Meg had to be satisfied. She lay awake a long time wondering about Julie. He'd have to settle down sooner or later, and somehow she sounded suitable.

She learnt a little more about her during dinner the following day; she had given the Professor his breakfast that morning, but beyond an exchange of good mornings they had had nothing to say to each other. But now he joined them for dinner wearing a dinner jacket.

'Did you have a good dinner?' enquired his grandmother.

'Excellent, my dear. Professor Tacx doesn't change—he must be getting on a bit, though.'

'Indeed, yes. And Julie? She was such a pretty child? I hear she loved the States.'

'She's become a beautiful young woman. I'm taking her dancing and out to supper.' He addressed the table at large, but his eyes were on Meg. She couldn't stop herself from looking at him, but encountered his hard stare, so she calmly looked away; he was comparing her in her familiar pink dress with the brilliant creature he would soon meet. She went pink with mortification.

She woke after a night broken with long periods of wakefulness. It was the last day. Tomorrow they would leave Amsterdam, and she was glad. She wasn't sure what she had expected, but she had been disappointed. She got up earlier than usual, anxious to have everything just so before Florence arrived back at midday, and on the pretext of having extra household chores asked Anna to take the Professor's breakfast. Although he didn't go out, she managed to avoid having her coffee as usual in the drawing-room with the excuse that she had some shopping to do.

Florence, fetched from the station by the Professor, declared everything to be perfect. While they saw to lunch together she said, 'Why don't you have a few hours off this afternoon? Go on the canal trip or do some shopping? I dare say no one thought to ask you if you wanted any time to yourself . . .'

'Professor Culver very kindly took me to the Rijksmuseum and the Dam and some other places one afternoon,' Meg told her. 'Do you suppose anyone would mind If I went out after lunch? Just for an hour or two? I've got dinner ready as far as possible, and all the shopping is done. Anna's been marvellous.'

'You go, miss. Mr Ralph will be going out after lunch, I'll be bound, and the two ladies will be resting. No need for you to come back before tea, either, though I'll be glad of a bit of help before dinner, I dare say.'

'I'll be back soon after five o'clock—would that be early enough?'

'That would do nicely. I don't like asking you really, miss—it doesn't seem right, you being a housekeeper, somehow.' Florence added, 'You being a young lady used to better things.'

Meg flushed. 'Well, I'm not really trained for anything, Florence, and I'm really very happy; I have a good job helping at the Professor's consulting rooms in London with my own little flat.'

'There's nothing like a home of your own, miss. Now, this evening— what did you have in mind for dinner?'

At lunch the talk was of their departure on the next day; they were to go by Hovercraft from Calais, leaving Amsterdam directly after breakfast. They should be home by teatime, declared the Professor; he would take his mother home and go on to Much Hadham with Meg to collect Nelson and make sure that everything there was as it should be. 'Work on Monday, Meg,' he warned her, and she smilingly agreed. She had been working all week, but he probably hadn't noticed that.

The two ladies went to their rooms after they had had coffee and the Professor went to the library at the back of the hall to telephone. Meg helped to clear the lunch dishes and then skipped to her room, changed into her Jaeger coat over a skirt and jumper and sped out of the house. Lunch had been a leisurely affair and she had less than three hours, but she knew exactly what she was going to do. She had noted the way they had walked when she had gone out with the Professor. She didn't go as far as the Rijksmuseum but turned off towards the Munt Plein and presently found herself in Kalverstraat. At one time, the Professor had told her, it had been the fashionable shopping street, but nowadays the shops were mostly for teenagers' gear mixed in with bookshops, one or two dress shops and some rather dark, sinister sex shops. Meg went the length of the street and came out on the Dam Plein. She crossed its patterned stones and went into the Bijenkorf, a kind of miniature Selfridges where she felt sure she would find something for her sisters as well as Miss Standish and Mary Giles. She had spent no money, and there were guilders enough in her purse.

After a lengthy search, she bought Delft Blue pottery for Doreen and Cora, small beribboned boxes of chocolates for Mrs Giles and Miss Standish, and a carton of Dutch cigars for Percy. For Betsy she chose more chocolates and a silk scarf and then, well pleased with her purchases, she took herself off to the nearby Damrak, purchased a ticket and got on one of the canal boats about to leave. It wasn't the best of days for sightseeing; there was a raw wind blowing and the sky was a uniform grey, but the boats were covered and warm. Meg sat with a couple of dozen other people and listened to the guide pointing out the sights in three languages. She arrived back at the landing stage stuffed with facts and information which she hoped she would be able to

remember. It had all been so quick—she had wanted to
linger by the old houses, and get more than a hurried
glimpse of the narrow canals branching away on every
side—but it had been marvellous all the same. She had
decided to have a cup of tea and take a taxi back, and sat
down in one of the cafés close to the Dam Palace. Tea
came in a glass with no milk, but the cake she had with it
more than made up for that. She would have liked to
have sat there for half an hour and watched the crowds
surging past, but it was time to go. She paid her bill,
found a taxi and arrived back with ten minutes to spare.

Anna opened the door to her, and as Meg went past
her into the hall the Professor came out of the drawing-
room. He stood in front of her so that she couldn't pass
him. 'Where have you been?' he asked her in what she
privately called his nasty voice. He was smiling a nasty
smile, too.

'I had the afternoon off, Professor Culver.'

'In other words, mind my own business, eh?'

She didn't answer him, and after a moment he said
half angrily, 'I thought we might do the canal trip this
evening—I said I would take you.'

She said gently, 'I went this afternoon. It was most
interesting.'

His eyes narrowed; they looked very black. He turned
on his heel and went back into the drawing-room, and
Meg went to her room and changed back into the grey
dress trying to guess why he had suddenly looked so
furiously angry.

There was plenty to do in the kitchen while Anna set
the table and Florence put the finishing touches to the
trifle. 'Mr Ralph always loved trifle,' she declared fondly.
'I always make him one when he comes to visit.'

'He comes often?' asked Meg.

'Bless you, yes. Seeing that he's such a busy gentleman,
you'd been surprised at the times he pops over just to

spend a night with his grandmother. Very fond of her, he is, like he is of his ma, too. Had his hands full, I reckon, since his grandfather and his father died; sees to all their business for them, and there's a lot of that, I can tell you, being that they're wealthy folk . . . And he's kind—he'll help anyone—does it unbeknownst, too—you'd be surprised at the jobs he's created just to give someone a chance to earn an honest living. There's that Percy in London and the gardener at Much Hadham and the men on the farm he owns in Friesland.'

You can add me to the list, thought Meg silently, and in a sudden spurt of rage decided there and then to start looking for another job as soon as they got back to London, although as the rage died she had to admit there were difficulties: where would she find a flat like the one she lived in now, and would she get a job such as the one she now had, and what about Nelson and the lodge and Lucky?

She changed into the pink dress and went along to the drawing-room to join everybody. The Professor was there, dispensing drinks. His politeness chilled her to the very marrow of her bones; there was no sign of his previous ill temper. The talk ranged from their journey on the morrow to comments upon Amsterdam and its charms. It was disconcerting when his grandmother said suddenly, 'You're a nice girl, Meg. You must come again, but of course you will, anyway.'

Probably she would, Meg agreed politely; she would like to see more of Holland and it was an easy journey— less than an hour's flying time. 'Not that I've ever flown,' she finished honestly.

Dinner was pleasant; the Professor exerted himself to be amicable and amusing. The food was delicious, and they sat over it in a leisurely way. It was as Meg was carrying the coffee tray into the drawing-room that Anna came to say that the Professor was wanted on the telephone. She was handing Mrs Culver her cup when he came back.

'Julie, asking if I'll go round for a drink and to say goodbye. You'll forgive me, Granny? I promise you I'll be back before you go to bed.'

He shook his head at Meg's offer of coffee, dropped a kiss on the old lady's cheek and went.

'I thought he said something about taking you on the canal trip this evening, dear?' remarked his mother.

'Nothing definite, Mrs Culver—and what a good thing we didn't go—he would have missed seeing his friends.' Meg's voice was as calm as usual. 'Besides, I went this afternoon; it was fascinating.'

They sat and talked until Mrs Culver said, 'Oh, I've still got my packing to do and I do so hate that.' She looked at Meg, who said at once, 'I'll do it for you, Mrs Culver. What do you want me to leave out for you to wear for the journey?'

She was glad to have something to do, so that she could shut her mind to Ralph. He wouldn't be back until late; the old lady went to bed at eleven o'clock each evening, but she didn't sleep until the small hours but sat up in bed and read. Meg knew that because she had taken hot drinks to her on two occasions. She finished Mrs Culver's packing and looked at her watch: it was eleven o'clock and the house was quiet. As she reached the door, Mrs Culver came in.

'Finished, dear? How kind you are! I'm going to bed, as we have to be away fairly early, don't we?'

They wished each other a good night and Meg went along to the drawing-room. The old lady would have gone to her room, too; she would just make sure the lights were out and the room fairly tidy before she went to the kitchen to see if Florence needed her help.

There was one small table lamp burning. The Professor was sitting in the dimness, doing nothing. He got to his feet as Meg stopped in surprise, and said, 'There you are—where have you been?'

'Packing for your mother, Professor. I came to turn off the lights, but perhaps you would do that when you go to bed?'

She turned to go and found him beside her, staring down into her face. 'Prim,' he said nastily, and 'A poker down your back,' and kissed her hard.

CHAPTER EIGHT

MEG rushed past him, quite forgetting that she had been going to help Florence in the kitchen, and once she was in her room she sat down on her bed, a prey to a multitude of strong feelings. Her head told her that she must ignore his kiss, although her heart denied that. She wasn't sure why he had kissed her. He could have had no pleasure from it; he had called her prim and poker-backed, and that was something she would always remember. She had been out of her mind to imagine he could become even a little interested in her.

She undressed like a whirlwind and jumped into bed, where she burst into tears; let Julie or that horrible girl in England get their dainty, devastating claws into him—he'd make a rotten husband anyway. She sniffed and snuffled for a long time before she went to sleep at last to wake early with a headache and a red nose from weeping. She showered and dressed and did her best to disguise her nose, and went along to the kitchen where Florence was already busy.

'I'm sorry about last night,' began Meg. 'I really did mean to come and give you a hand, but I—I got delayed.'

Florence had taken a look at her face. 'Don't you worry, miss—Anna came in early and we had everything cleared up in no time. If you'd take in Mrs Culver's tea? I won't disturb the mistress for a bit but I'll get a tray ready for them both.' She glanced at the clock. 'There isn't all that much time, and Mr Ralph wants to leave not a minute after nine o'clock.'

Mrs Culver grumbled a little when Meg woke her. 'So

early,' she moaned. 'I can't think why Ralph couldn't leave later in the day; surely he need not work on Monday.' She glanced at Meg and then looked again. 'My dear, are you all right? You look as though you haven't slept a wink. What a selfish woman I am; you must have been up hours ago!' She sat up in bed and said contritely, 'Tell me what I can do to help.' And then added helplessly, 'I'll never be ready to leave, and Ralph will be annoyed.'

Meg poured her tea. 'If you take your bath as soon as you've had your tea, I'll bring your breakfast tray, then all you have to do is to dress. I'll finish your packing.'

'You are a treasure! Tea and toast, dear, and some of that black cherry jam . . .'

Florence had set the table for two, and the idea of being at breakfast with the Professor gave Meg cold feet, but if she had absented herself from it he would know that she minded what he had said, and that was the last thing she wanted. He was already at table, but he got to his feet as she sat down, wished her a good morning in his usual rather cool manner, passed her the toast and offered the coffee pot.

She wasn't hungry, but she did her best, exchanging casual remarks with him with her usual calm until with a glance at her watch she excused herself.

'Escaping, Meg?' he asked blandly.

'No—I'm going to take Mrs Culver her breakfast. She's anxious not to keep you waiting.' She gave him a small, tolerant smile as she got up from the table, her lovely eyes wide and innocent. 'And what is there for me to escape from?'

She closed the door gently on his rumble of laughter.

They left at nine o'clock precisely. Meg had gone spare getting Mrs Culver into her hat and coat, finding her handbag, her passport and the pills she needed in case she felt queasy on the journey. She had packed the last of her cases and then gone to say goodbye to the Professor's grandmother, sitting up in bed, wrapped in a white cobweb shawl.

A small bony hand beckoned her to the bedside. 'You're a good girl, and a splendid housekeeper. You've not had the pleasure a young woman should have at your age, but it'll come—it'll come. You may kiss me.'

Which Meg, did, rather surprised, for she hadn't thought that the old lady had noticed her more than good manners expected of her.

'I'm glad Florence had her holiday and that I could help out', Meg smiled. 'She's a marvellous person, isn't she? I've enjoyed being here, and I shall think of you.' She kissed the soft old cheek.

'Send that grandson of mine in here, will you?' called the old lady after her as she left.

The Professor was loading the luggage into the boot. In the early morning sunlight he looked remarkably handsome. Meg sighed with silent longing and gave him his grandmother's message, and then went to urge Mrs Culver to get into the car.

The Professor entered his grandparent's room quietly and went to sit on the edge of the bed. 'Not long enough, was it, Granny?' he asked cheerfully. 'I'll come over at Easter for a couple of days.'

The bright old eyes behind the gold-rimmed spectacles studied his impassive face. 'Do that, my dear; I enjoyed these few days. That girl of yours is a treasure.'

He agreed amiably. 'Yes, isn't she, but she's not my girl, Granny.'

She put her small hand in his large one. 'I look forward to seeing you, Ralph.' She chuckled gently. 'Wasn't Julie the one, my dear?'

'No, Granny. I think I'm impossible to please.'

'There's no such word as impossible. Don't forget to say goodbye to Nanny.'

The motorway was fairly empty, and the Rolls made light of the miles; they stopped for coffee and Meg was glad of the half-hour in the wayside café. She had been sitting in front and the Professor had proved difficult to talk to. In fact she had given up after a series of monosyllabic answers to her observations, and on the short way back to the car she had asked him if he would prefer to have his mother sitting beside him.

'Good God, no! Sitting in the back she can't see the speedometer; anything over fifty miles an hour gives her palpitations.'

They had more coffee and sandwiches on the Hovercraft once they had boarded it at Calais and, once free of Customs, they drove up the M2, through the Blackwall Tunnel and the Ring Road and so northwards to Hertfordshire. He had said that they would be home by teatime, and they were.

Meg's old home looked charming as he stopped before its door. The garden had been restored to its former pristine condition and was a blaze of daffodils and early tulips. And there was Betsy, opening the door to them, and Kate coming forward to welcome them.

They had tea in the drawing-room, with a log fire blazing and Silky weaving his way from one to the other of them, but they didn't linger. Commenting that he would telephone his mother within the next day or so, the Professor urged Meg out to the car and drove to his own home.

Meg craned her neck as they went past the lodge. The garden looked lovely; the daffodils were out there too and the primroses she had cherished were a yellow carpet under the hedge. The window boxes and flower beds round the house were even more colourful. She paused to

look at them as she got out of the car and was almost
knocked flat on to her back by Lucky, who had raced out
of the door Trugg was holding open. The bull terriers
were more dignified, and they made for the Professor.

Mrs Trugg came into the hall as they went in, beaming
at the sight of them, wanting to know if they would like a
meal and if the journey had been a good one.

'No meal,' said the Professor, 'and we had tea at my
mother's. We must be on our way.'

'Then you'll want Nelson—he's all ready, and won't he
be pleased to see you? He's been so good, but he's missed
you, miss. Trugg shall fetch him. You'll be down at the
weekend, sir?'

The Professor was leafing through his post. 'Yes, Mrs
Trugg. I may be coming down one evening during the
week; I'll let you know.'

Nelson, dignified in his box, allowed Meg to hug him
before he was stowed in the back of the car. Lucky
wanted to get in too.

'Not now, Lucky!' Meg hated to leave him again. 'But
I'll see you at the weekend.'

She got into the car and sat quietly while the Professor
bade his dogs goodbye, told Lucky to be good and
exchanged a few words with Trugg and then got in beside
her and drove off.

Meg had plently to think about; she would feed Nelson
as soon as she got in, get herself a supper of sorts, unpack
and put things ready for the morning. She would have to
phone Doreen and Cora too; the evening wasn't going to
be long enough. She was jolted out of her plans by the
Professor's voice. 'I'll be in early in the morning, Meg. Be
ready by half past eight, will you?'

'Yes, Professor.'

They lapsed into silence once again until they reached
the consulting rooms.

'Thank you for fetching Nelson,' said Meg politely, 'and for bringing me back. I—I enjoyed my stay in Holland.'

The Professor said 'Ha,' in a fierce way and got out of the car. He undid his door and collected Nelson and her suitcase. 'Lead the way,' he said.

The flat felt cold and unlived-in. He closed its front door, put Nelson down, took her case through to the bedroom and bent to light the gas fire. Meg was trying to decide whether to ask him if he would like a cup of coffee when he said, 'If you give this animal his supper, we'll be on our way.'

Meg turned to look at him. 'Where to?' she asked.

'My house, of course—where else? Rosie will have a meal ready for us.'

Meg started to unbutton her coat. 'Professor Culver, I'm sure you mean to be kind, but I find you a litte overbearing. I wasn't aware until this moment that I was to have my supper with you. I should have liked to have been asked.'

'So that you could think up some sensible reason why you shouldn't accept! Your opinion of me may be low, my girl, but I hope I still have a vestige of good manners left. Do you expect me to leave you here, opening baked beans and finding milkless tea?'

'Well, yes—I did rather. You've been in a bad temper all day,' she went on in a matter-of-fact voice, 'and I thought you'd want to be rid of me as soon as possible.'

He went past her into the kitchen and opened a cupboard, found a tin of cat food and started to open it. Only when Nelson had bowed his elderly head over his plate did he say, 'I'm sorry.' He didn't say why he was angry. 'Shall we cry pax for the rest of the evening?'

He loomed over her, his handsome face full of tired lines, and just for one moment her heart wasn't curbed by her cautious tongue. 'Oh, my dear, you're tired to death,' she said impulsively. 'How thoughtless I am—of course I'll come, you'll feel so much better when you've had a nice meal ... all those miles and an early start this morning.'

She switched off the kitchen light and didn't see the look in his eyes as he watched her, her plain and earnest face tired too. She was still as neat as when they had set out that morning, only the tip of her small nose shone powderless now, and she had forgotten to put on more lipstick.

He smiled, and the tiredness was swept away. He turned the fire down low, switched off all but one table lamp, and then buttoned her coat again.

Meg stood like a small statue, her arms rigid in case she should throw them around his neck. Which would never do! She bade Nelson goodbye, told him to be a good boy and was swept downstairs again and into the car.

Rosie was waiting for them. If she was surprised to see Meg there was nothing in her face to show it; when the Professor had taken Meg's coat she led her away to tidy herself, shaking her head over the length of their journey. 'There's no stopping the Professor,' she confided to Meg. 'Always on the go, he is; he needs a wife to keep him at his own fireside and see that he eats proper meals.' She gave an indignant snort. 'And I don't mean those haughty types who swan in and out of the best restaurants. Bless the man, he deserves better than that.'

Meg, doing things to her face, agreed silently; what was more, she was going to work at it, hopeless though it seemed.

She sipped the sherry he gave her warily; her insides were empty and she wasn't sure what would happen if she tossed it back. She sat rather primly opposite him, watching him with his whisky and soda, striving to make light conversation.

He said rather impatiently, 'Mrs James and Nancy will be coming in the morning. The child's had her treatment, and now she's to stay at home for a couple of weeks before she goes to Maud's again.'

Meg perceived that his mind was already busy with the following day; small talk was the last thing he wanted. She asked, 'And was it successful, the treatment?'

He began to tell her about it, and she listened carefully; a good deal of what he was saying was way above her head but she did her best to understand. He stopped suddenly in mid-sentence. 'You've not understood the half of it, have you? I must beg your pardon for boring you.' He added with a surprised annoyance, 'I can't think why I should want to tell you all this.'

'Well,' said Meg sensibly, 'you need to talk about your work, and I'm here—I expect if I were your mother or one of your—your girl-friends you'd do just the same.'

'Good Lord, no! Certainly not my mother, and anyone else would be bored to tears.'

Which made her even more determined to rescue him from some selfish, uncaring wife. But to be determined wasn't enough . . .

'What are you plotting?' asked the Professor suddenly.

'Plotting? Me? Nothing. Would you explain exactly what high-speed neutrons and pi mesons are?'

He put down his drink and sat forward in his chair. 'You really want to know?'

When she nodded he told her, using simple language which she could understand, and he was only interrupted by Rosie coming to tell them that dinner was ready.

Meg was famished; she would have welcomed food of any sort to still the rumblings of her insides. The Tomates Suisses with which Rosie served them were delicious, but the tomatoes stuffed with cream cheese and chives, while absolutely delectable, did little more than take the edge off her appetite. She sighed with relieved delight when a deep earthenware dish of Boeuf Bourguignon was placed before the Professor, and her nose wrinkled appreciatively at the delicious aroma of steak and pork and onions and the tang of the red wine in which they had been cooking for hours.

The Professor gravely pressed her to a second helping and talked casually of nothing in particular while he watched her with a genuine gleam of amusement.

Chocolate orange mousse ended their meal, and Meg, who was no mean cook herself, observed seriously, 'Your housekeeper is a Cordon Bleu cook, isn't she? Would you mind if I told her how much I've enjoyed my dinner?' She added, 'I was so hungry!'

He said in a voice as bland as his face, 'Rosie will be delighted to hear it. I'm afraid I seldom remember to tell her how excellent her cooking is. Shall we have coffee in the drawing-room?'

Meg could have stayed for hours, sitting by the fire in the comfortable room over coffee, not talking much, utterly content just to be with the Professor. But she had seen the great pile of letters on the hall table as they had entered the house and he would want to read them in peace—and probably telephone that horrid girl to tell her that he was back again, whispered a small voice at the back of her head. After half an hour she said, 'I think I should go Professor—unpacking and Nelson and things . . . it's been lovely.'

'My pleasure, Meg.' All of a sudden he was coolly impassive and made no effort to keep her.

Nelson's ecstatic welcome couldn't disperse the loneliness of the flat once the Professor had dropped her there and gone. Meg unpacked, made ready for the morning, bustling around so that she had no chance to think too much, and then went to bed. In the morning she would see him again, but it wouldn't be at all the same thing.

He was punctual, but Miss Standish and Mrs Giles were ahead of him; Meg had time to give them her small presents and run down to the basement with the cigars for Percy. When he came he was pleasantly friendly to everyone, and a little remote. Certainly there was little warmth in his manner toward Meg; she had been treasuring the memory of their pleasant evening together, but apparently he had dismissed it as an obligatory invitation which good manners had compelled him to make. She assumed her self-effacing image without loss of time.

The day unwound itself briskly; Mrs James and Nancy were the first of the patients, and when they had gone and Meg was filing away the notes, she sneaked a look at them. The Professor's writing was atrocious, and it took her a minute or two to discover that he was satisfied with the child's progress and that she was to go back for further treatment in a few days' time. Mrs James had been tearful but quiet, and Nancy, unaware that the Professor was pitting his brilliant brain against her illness, skipped around the waiting-room, chattering happily to Meg.

It was a good beginning to the day; patients came and went and just before lunch the Professor left for the hospital. He wouldn't be back until three o'clock, so that Mrs Giles left soon after, and then Miss Standish for her lunch hour. Meg tidied up ready for the afternoon and went up to the flat to share a snack meal with Nelson, do her hand-washing and daydream. The phone interrupted her; Doreen, wanting to know why she hadn't telephoned as soon as she got back. Meg gave her a brief account of her stay in Amsterdam, not mentioning the dinner with the Professor, and on the plea of being busy rang off, with the promise that she would ring again later.

By the end of the day it was just as though she had never been away; she took up the reins of her uneventful days and the week went by. She could have counted on two hands the number of times the Professor had spoken to her, but she refused to be discouraged by that. She saw him each day, and there was the weekend to look forward to.

Towards the end of the week he went to Bristol to give a lecture, and the three of them were more or less free until he returned in the late afternoon to see a patient. Meg, with a couple of hours to herself, took a bus to Harrods and bought a soft suede jacket to go with the Jaeger skirt. She bought shoes too, and then hurried back before she spent too much money.

She showed them to Miss Standish when she got back in and waltzed around the waiting-room, trying them on. But by the time the Professor got back, she was sitting at her desk, neat and demure, giving the strong impression that she didn't want anyone to notice her.

It wasn't until Friday evening that he stopped on his way out to say, 'You'd like to go to the lodge for the weekend, Meg? I'll pick you up just after one o'clock.'

It was a rush to be ready; the last patient had taken up a lot of time. Meg rushed upstairs to the flat, bolted cheese and biscuits while she flung a few things into her ovenight bag, changed into the skirt and the new jacket and shoes, and popped Nelson in the new basket she had brought for him. She was closing the front door behind her as the Professor drew up, and a couple of minutes later, with her bag and Nelson in the back, she was sitting beside him as he started on the now familiar journey.

She sensed that he didn't want to talk. They were

almost there when he said, 'You are the only woman I know who doesn't chatter, Meg.' He added in a voice which she didn't much care for, 'Sometimes I wonder what you're thinking about.'

A good thing he had no idea, she reflected silently. 'Oh, this and that,' he was told airily, and she lapsed into her usual self-imposed silence once more.

He got out at the lodge gate, opened the door for her and put Nelson and her bag inside. 'About six o'clock tomorrow evening?' he warned her, and drove off. She watched the car disappear round the corner of the drive; he had become remote during the past week and she couldn't help but notice that it was only with her. With Miss Standish and Mrs Giles he had been exactly as he always was. As far as she knew she had done her work well enough and she had been careful not to take advantage of his various kindnesses—on the contrary. She went back into the cottage and plunged into the pleasant business of putting it to rights before Lucky should arrive. It was Trugg who brought him, and he stayed to chat for a few minutes, letting fall the information that there would be weekend guests up at the house.

'Oh, that will be nice for Profesor Culver; he needs to relax after a busy week.' Meg spoke lightly and smiled widely, mentally tearing the blonde girl limb from limb.

She had been to Much Hadham and done her shopping with Lucky, and was poking round the garden when a red sports car went past. The girl was driving and there was no one with her, and hard on her heels came a second car, a big BMW with four people in it. Meg went indoors and put the kettle on and presently sat down to her tea. She had lit the fire and she sat on long after she had finished, watching the flames and wondering what the Professor was doing.

He was entertaining his guests with his usual impeccable good manners and thinking about her.

It was almost light when Meg woke the next morning, but still early. Something had woken her, and she sat up in bed and listened; someone was trying to get a car to go, out in the road, near the gate, and she hopped out of bed, put on her dressing gown and slippers and went to look from the living-room window. Whoever it was sounded desperate, and above the banging and clanking she could hear a soft moaning. Nelson and Lucky were still more or less asleep by the fire; Meg unlocked the door and went round the corner of the drive to the road.

There was a down-at-heel car parked on the verge with its bonnet open and a man with his head and shoulders inside it. The moans were definitely coming from inside the car and Meg tapped him on the arm. 'What's wrong?'

He was a young man with a very worried face. 'My wife—I'm taking her to hospital at Bishop's Stortford, but the car's broken down and she's sure the baby's coming!'

Meg looked at his white face and poked her head through the car window. There was a young woman on the back seat, tears streaming down her cheeks. She said weakly, 'Do help me—I know the baby's almost here and I'm so cold!'

'Can you manage to walk just a few yards?' Meg turned to speak to the man, who had given up on the car and was standing beside her. A nice enough lad, she considered, but not very able to cope. 'Will you carry your wife into the lodge; it's just inside that entrance gate. I'll go and see to the bed.'

She didn't wait to see if he agreed but sped to the lodge, flung a sheet over the bedclothes and piled the blankets on a chair. Bed, she thought in a panic, seemed the best place. She shut the animals in the kitchen and held the door wide for the man to come in. The girl was terrified as well as cold. Meg took off the coat she was wearing on top of her dressing gown and nightie, piled blankets on to her, bade the man to stay and ran to the house. Six o'clock in the morning wasn't an ideal time to bang on people's doors, but she had to have help.

The house was quiet, just tinged by the light in the sky, a chilly little wind blowing through the trees surrounding it. Meg rushed to the door, rang the bell and banged on the big brass knocker. She kept her finger on the bell until she heard sounds of movement inside and almost fell into the hall, when Trugg, cosily wrapped in a dressing gown, opened the door.

He put out a hand to steady her, closed the door and asked anxiously, 'What's the matter, Miss Collins? Come into the sitting-room and sit down . . .'

'No time, Trugg, I want Professor Culver . . .'

'A matter of some urgency?' asked the Professor from the staircase.

Even in a dressing gown and pyjamas he looked capable of dealing with any situation, however outlandish.

'You must come at once,' said Meg, not mincing her words. 'There's a woman in the lodge—the car broke down, she's having a baby and I'm not sure what to do.' She added fiercely. 'You're a doctor . . .'

The Professor smiled faintly. It was quite some years since, as a medical student, he had delivered a baby. 'I'll get my bag,' he said calmly, and a moment later was striding down the drive with Meg trotting along beside him.

The next hour or so was so packed with action that Meg had no idea of what was happening. The Professor, exuding confidence and calm, reassured the girl, assessed the situation without fuss, suggested that the man should sit by the wife and hold her hand, and issued orders to Meg in an unhurried voice as though delivering babies in his lodge was something he was accustomed to do as a matter of course.

Presently Meg found herself holding out a folded blanket to receive a baby boy, yelling with gratifying vigour.

'Give him to his mother—hold those forceps,' the Professor demanded, and then with well-held impatience, 'hold them still . . .'

Meg resisted a desire to cast everything down and rush out of the cottage. She was icy cold, faintly queasy and she had just come through the fright of her life. She sniffed back tears and clenched her teeth.

'Right,' said the Professor, 'let go now. Will you make us all a cup of tea?'

She went without a word into the kitchen and put the kettle on, and while it was boiling gave Nelson and Lucky their breakfasts. When she took the tea-tray back into the bedroom the Professor was sitting on the side of the bed, discussing suitable names for the baby. She loved him to distraction, but just then she could have boxed his ears.

She poured tea for everyone, listening to the the man and his wife's happy voices repeating their thanks over and over again. She finished her tea and became aware that the Professor was watching her.

'If you've finished, Meg, will you go to the house and get Trugg to phone for an ambulance? Tell him to say it's urgent, and then ring the hospital and tell them that Mrs Pitt is on the way with a newborn infant.' As she went out of the door, he added, 'And put on a coat or something— you'll catch your death of cold!'

A bit late in the day for that, she muttered, and flung an old mac she kept for Lucky's walk over her shoulders.

Trugg was hovering in the hall, and the door was opened before she could ring the bell. The ambulance was called and he got the hospital number for her and then handed her the telephone.

'Who's speaking?' asked the voice at the other end.

'Meg Collins on behalf of Professor Culver; the baby was born in his cottage. He delivered it.'

The voice warmed. 'Will you tell him that we'll be quite ready? Will he be coming with the patient?'

'I don't know. I'll ask him to phone you as soon as he can leave Mrs Pitt.'

Trugg looked at her with fatherly concern. 'You didn't ought to run around like that, miss—catch your death, you will! Come to the kitchen and Mrs Trugg will give you a nice hot drink.'

'I think the Professor expects me to go straight back, thank you, Trugg. I hope I didn't wake everyone?'

'Well, miss, there was a modicum of grumbling, but tea has been taken to everyone and I dare say that by now they're all sleeping.' His voice held no expression.

'Well, thank you, Trugg.' Meg went to the door and he pushed it open for her. 'Trugg,' she hesitated, 'the Professor will be cold and tired when he gets back—I can't suggest it to him, but he'll listen to you—if you could get him to put on some warm clothes and eat his breakfast?'

Trugg smiled all over his face. 'Don't worry, miss; Mrs Trugg and I'll see that he does just that.'

'Thank you, Trugg.'

'Thank *you*, miss, and if I might say so, you could do with the same treatment.'

The Professor was still sitting on Mrs Pitt's bed when she got back. The room showed signs of upheaval, and she thought unhappily of the work which lay ahead of her. She took off the mac and collected the mugs after assuring the Professor that the ambulance was on its way and the hospital had been warned. She was so cold that the mugs rattled on the tray as she carried it out to the kitchen.

When the ambulance men came she shook hands with Mr and Mrs Pitt and then retired to a corner out of everyone's way. The baby was still yelling; she had peered at him, wrapped in his blankets, and his small fist had unfolded and caught her finger and gripped it tightly. She had smiled widely and the Professor, watching her, smiled too.

The ambulance slid away and Meg fetched a plastic rubbish bag and started cramming it with the bed linen. It surprised her very much when the Professor took it from her and finished the job. 'I'll take this up to the house with me and send Winnie the housemaid down to give you a hand,' he said, and when she protested, 'Don't argue with me. And have a hot shower and get into some clothes.' He was going through the door when he paused to say, 'You did very well.' His voice held warmth. 'But then I wouldn't have expected otherwise.'

At the door of his house, Trugg, still hovering, took the plastic bag from him with an annoyed 'Tut tut,' and the Professor, who wasn't a man to laugh very often laughed now. 'Ask Winnie to go down to the lodge and give Miss Collins a hand, will you, Trugg?'

'At once, Mr Ralph. And the young lady told me to see that you had a good hot shower and dressed warmly and ate a good breakfast.'

His master stood staring at him. 'Did she indeed?' He smiled slowly. 'Trugg, tell Winnie to see that Miss Collins comes up here for her breakfast—do you suppose Mrs Trugg could give us a meal in say, half an hour? No one will be down for hours yet, will they?'

'Half an hour, sir, and I'll send Winnie down at once.'

Meg was putting clean sheets on the bed when Winnie arrived.

'What a thing to happen, miss, so early in the morning, too!

Now you're to have your shower and dress and go up to the house for your breakfast. Half an hour, the master said. I'll soon have this place put to rights—you must be frozen to the bone. I'd have been scared . . .'

'Well, I was. Thank you, Winnie, but have you the time to spare?'

'Lor' bless you, miss, there's Mary up at the house to carry the trays to the rooms. I had my breakfast an hour ago.'

Meg, warmer now and wearing the skirt and new jacket over her sweater, warned Winnie to keep an eye on the animals, and hurried up to the house a minute or two late. The Professor opened the door to her, swept her into the dining-room and sat her down at the table. 'That's better, though I must say you looked rather nice *en déshabillé*, even if distraught.'

She went pink. 'I didn't have time to dress,' she began.

'No—I was glad of that.' He spoke with a gravity which belied the gleam in his eyes, and went on briskly as Trugg put a covered dish before him. 'Now, eggs, bacon, mushrooms, tomatoes, fried bread . . . Mrs Trugg seems to think we need feeding up!'

The food was delicious, as was the coffee, and they didn't hurry. But a glance at the clock set Meg on her feet. 'I must go—thank you for my lovely breakfast and for sending Winnie.'

He went to the door with her. 'I'm going to Bishop's Stortford this afternoon, just a follow-up visit—I'd like you to come with me.'

'Your guests . . .?'

'They can come too if they wish, but I think it most

unlikely. I'll collect you just before two o'clock.' He bent
and kissed her cheek and said softly, 'Please, Meg?' So
that she said hastily,

'Yes, all right, I'll come.'

The lodge was in apple-pie order when she got back.
She soothed Nelson's ruffled feelings, took Lucky for a
walk and got herself lunch.

The Professor arrived five minutes early; he banged on
the door and stalked in. 'I've got Ben and Polly with me,
and there's no reason why Lucky shouldn't come too; we
shall only be away for an hour.'

A remark which Meg received with regret.

It was barely four miles to Bishop Stortford. The
Professor parked the car in the consultants' car park, and
at Meg's look said, 'I've friends here.' He marched her in
and up to the Maternity Unit.

Mrs Pitt was in a corner bed, and now that all the
hassle was over, she looked a very pretty girl. Meg had
picked a bunch of spring flowers from the garden; she
offered them and then went to the foot of the bed to
admire the infant Pitt in his cot, leaving the Professor to
talk to Mrs Pitt, until Sister came rustling down the ward
and he wandered off with her with a quick excuse. He
wasn't gone for more than five minutes, and when he
came back he suggested that Mr Pitt might like a stroll in
the hospital grounds.

Which left Meg and Mrs Pitt quite happily discussing
baby clothes and the best sort of pram. 'Not that we can
buy one,' said Mrs Pitt. 'Ned's out of work and our
landlord's putting up the rent next week.'

'What will you do?' asked Meg. Perhaps they would
accept some money, a loan even; she could spare enough
to keep them going for a time . . .

'Our luck is bound to change,' declared Mrs Pitt,
uttering, if she did but know it, the truth.

They didn't stay long; the Professor seemed in a hurry to get back home. He looked smug, thought Meg, studying his face when he wasn't looking.

She was getting out of the car at the lodge when the red sports car flashed past and she said, 'Oh, there's one of your guests . . . the girl.'

He got out too and opened the door for Lucky. 'She's leaving. We said goodbye. Come up for tea at half past four, Meg—I'd like you to meet my friends.'

'I'd rather not, if you don't mind.'

'But I do mind. You'll like them.'

He got back into the car and drove off without waiting for her to answer.

Meg took Lucky for a walk, made sure that the cottage was tidy and ready for the following week, and reluctantly went up to the house.

The Professor seemed determined to show his charming side; she was introduced to the four people in the drawing-room and skilfully put at her ease. Old friends, explained the Professor blandly; they had been students together. The wives were friendly, neither of them particularly pretty but both well dressed. The talk was easy and Meg found herself liking them, at the same time feeling surprised; they didn't seem at all the kind of young women the Professor would take to. She had a fleeting memory of the girl with the fair hair, so unlike his four other guests.

She didn't stay long, and shortly after she was back at the lodge she heard the car go past and got ready to leave. Trugg came for Lucky presently, and then minutes later the Professor arrived, still blandly friendly but thoughtful too.

At his consulting rooms he carried Nelson up to the flat and then stood in the middle of the room saying nothing, so that Meg asked him hesitantly if he would like a cup of coffee. And when he refused she said, 'I'm glad Mrs Pitt's all right. How lucky that the car broke down at your gateway.' She added, 'He's out of work and the landlord is puting up his rent. Did you know that?'

'Yes, we had a little chat.' He sat down and said, 'I'll have that coffee after all, Meg.'

She made good coffee; they emptied the pot between them and half an hour passed like lightning. The Professor put himself out to be charming and Meg felt happiness welling up inside her. She didn't only love him, she liked him too, and just for the moment he was giving her the impression that he liked her as well.

He got to his feet reluctantly. 'I've a mass of work to do,' he told her. 'I have no wish to go, but I must.'

She walked with him to the door, and hoped that he would kiss her again. He didn't, but as he turned to go he said casually, 'Pitt is a farm labourer; I've taken him on as a gardener. They can have the lodge to live in. I'll be free on Wednesday afternoon and I'll drive you down so that you can pack up your odds and ends. Trugg will store them for you in the attic.'

He lifted a casual hand and ran downstairs, leaving her with a very white face, staring into a suddenly disrupted future.

CHAPTER NINE

MEG closed the door slowly and rather blindly collected the coffee tray and took it into the kitchen. She fed Nelson, washed the mugs and unpacked her bag, and only when she had done this did she sit down to think.

Of course it made sense, The Profesor had offered her the cottage until such time as he should want it for a gardener; to him, with his delightful home in Little Venice and his still lovelier home at Much Hadham, it would seem a trivial enough matter. After all, her home was here. She caught her breath and sat up very straight; or was it? He could sack her any day he liked and she would have to move, find herself somewhere to live and get another job. He wouldn't do that; he was, under that chilly manner, a kind man. He hadn't been very kind to her, though . . . On the other hand he had given a much-needed helping hand to the Pitts; they needed a home and work and he had offered both. Something she had been trying not to think about persisted at the back of her head. Perhaps the girl had made him do it; perhaps if she was going to marry the Professor, she had objected to Meg being in the lodge. She was a beautiful girl, thought Meg wistfully, and the Professor had demonstrated only too clearly that she had no occasion to feel even a twinge of jealousy.

She sniffed back a threatening tear and addressed Nelson. 'And I actually thought I could do something about it! I thought I could compete with her, and look where it's got me . . . And if she doesn't like the idea of me spending the weekend at the lodge, she most certainly won't like me living here!'

Nelson climbed rather stiffly on to her lap and butted her with his elderly head, and she gave him a hug which he suffered with silent dignity. 'We'd better start looking at flats,' she told him, and went to get the supper she didn't want.

Monday proved to be like all other Mondays: a tight schedule of patients and hospitals and a great many phone calls. The Professor was no different; he greeted her with his normal cool affability, drank the coffee she took in to him and started on his day's work. There was no mention of the lodge and she hadn't expected it; possibly he had dismissed the whole matter from his mind. Once work was over for the day she repaired to her flat, made a pot of strong tea and worked her way through the 'To Let' advertisments in the evening paper. She had read through a whole page of convenient flats, described in rosy terms and offered at fabulous rents, when Doreen phoned.

She was a Ward Sister now and had a great deal to say about it, so beyond asking Meg if she was well she asked few questions, which was a good thing, for Meg had decided not to say a word to either of her sisters. She would wait and see what was to happen; she couldn't be turned out at a moment's notice. She would have time to find somewhere to live and a job of some sort. Besides, she would have a reference now, and that would help.

Of course the Professor might want her to stay; the weekends at the lodge had been a kindly gesture and she supposed she had taken it for granted that there would never be a gardener. It was ironic that in befriending the Pitts she had done herself a disservice. Self-pity would get her nowhere; she had a home, no financial worry and a job she enjoyed. And Nelson, of course. She would miss Lucky, but he had a good home and Ben and Polly for

company and she could explore London each weekend—
and there were the parks.

Tuesday was as busy as Monday, but when the last
patient had gone on Wednesday morning and they were
clearing up after the morning's consulting, the Professor
put his head round the waiting-room door.

'I'll be back at half past one, Meg.' He didn't wait for
an answer.

'Going out, dear?' asked Miss Standish, and looked
coy.

Mrs Giles was there too, so it seemed a good
opportunity to explain about the lodge.

'You'll miss it, Meg,' observed Mrs Giles. 'Luckily it's
spring and the parks are beginning to look lovely—and
you've got the dear little flat.'

'Oh, there's a lot of London I must see,' said Meg
cheerfully. 'Sunday is a nice day for wandering about. Of
course I shall miss the lodge, but it will be a perfect home
for the Pitts. The Professor's going to his home this
afternoon and he's giving me a lift so that I can collect my
bits and pieces. The Pitts are moving in at the weekend.'

She closed the door on her colleagues and ran upstairs;
there wasn't much time and the Professor hated to be
kept waiting.

She was waiting on the doorstep as he drew up, armed
with a large shopping basket; there would be things to
bring back with her, although she intended leaving pots
and pans and the cheap china she had bought for the
cottage.

She asked in her sensible way, 'How long may I have to
pack up? There isn't much ...'

He said impatiently, 'A couple of hours at least. Trugg
will fetch whatever you want to store—he can take the
Range Rover. I suggest that you don't bring too much
back to the flat.'

All her worried guesses came crowding back, but she said quietly, 'No, I won't—only some bits of china and silver.'

He grunted a reply and the rest of the journey was accomplished in silence.

It was a fine afternoon after a rainy morning; the cottage sparkled in the sunshine and its little garden had repaid all Meg's hard work with a display of tulips and daffodils and forget-me-nots. She got out of the car, silently shaking her head at the Professor's offer to go in with her, and then she turned the key in the door and went inside. The little room looked inviting, and the sun had warmed it. She stood a minute looking around her, filled with regret at having to leave it, then she took off her jacket, fetched a duster and started packing the small ornaments. It took no time at all; she put the basket on the table and took down the pictures she had brought with her from home. There were only the little work table and prayer chair to go into the attic. She dusted them lovingly, wondering if she could take them back with her to that flat; they would go in the boot . . .

Lucky's happy bark sent her to the door, to find Trugg there.

'Is this all, miss?' he wanted to know. 'No call for the Range Rover—leave them there, and I'll take them up this evening. I thought you'd like to have Lucky for an hour, miss, and Professor Culver says will you come up to the house for tea—half past four.'

It was already three o'clock and she hesitated. Trugg said, 'He'd be glad of the company, miss.'

'All right, Trugg. I'd love to come. I'll take Lucky for a walk and just make sure that everything's all right here.'

Left alone once more, and with Lucky in close attendance, she turned out drawers and cupboards, leaving anything Mrs Pitt might find useful; she left tea

and sugar too and a tin of milk and a couple of tins of
soup and a packet of biscuits. She wished she could have
been there to see the Pitts' happy faces when they moved
in.

She crossed the road presently and walked briskly
along the bridle path which would take her to Penny
Green; there wasn't time to go the whole way, and she
turned regretfully and went back past the lodge to the
house.

The Professor came out of his study as Trugg admitted
her. He had Ben and Polly at his heels, and they came to
greet her and then tangled happily with Lucky. 'Packed
up?' asked the Professor in what Meg considered to be a
heartless manner. 'Let's have tea.'

Mrs Trugg had old-fashioned ideas about afternoon
tea. There were tiny sandwiches, toasted muffins
swimming in butter, a large fruit cake and a plate of little
chocolate cakes. Megg, asked to pour out, did so and,
being a sensible girl, made a good tea. Love, she had
discovered, had made no difference to her appetite.

The Professor talked idly, mostly about her old home,
and presently she realised that he was questioning her
closely. Did she miss it? Would she rather live in the
country than in London? Would she enjoy living in
London if she led a different life—theatres and dining
out and so on?

She answered him as honestly as she could. 'Well, I
should think it would be lovely if one could have a bit of
both. She added ingeniously, 'You have, haven't you?'

'Indeed, yes. I look forward to sharing my life with
someone who will appreciate it.'

There was a lead weight in Meg's chest. She said
inanely, 'Oh, how nice,' and mentally consigned the
blonde girl to the bottom of the sea. They had made it up;
perhaps the Professor liked to live in a constant state of

dispute and reconciliation, and probably the girl was tender and loving towards him, although she found that hard to stomach. She asked with false brightness, 'You're getting married, Professor?'

'I do have that in mind. I suppose we should be going—I have a dinner date.'

She stopped herself in time from saying, 'How nice,' again. Instead she jumped to her feet with eagerness which made him lift his brows, said goodbye to the dogs, lingering over Lucky, for she might never see him again, and walked briskly into the hall where Trugg was waiting. She said goodbye to him too, then got into the car feeling as though her small world was falling apart around her. Any minute now, she reflected, and he would tell her in his cool way that he no longer required her services at his consulting rooms.

But he didn't; he carried on a desultory conversation about gardening in general and the garden at Much Hadham in particular. They were back in London without anything of significance having been said. Meg made haste to get out of the car, fearful that he might deal her a last-minute blow.

He got out too, carried her basket of odds and ends up to the flat and bade her a pleasant good evening.

It seemed strange, when Saturday came round, not being in a hurry to get ready to leave for the lodge. Meg changed into her outdoor things and took the bus to the Victoria and Albert Museum, but, interesting though it was, it was a poor substitute for Much Hadham; she wandered round for an hour and then went in search of a tea shop. London on a Saturday afternoon had closed its doors until Monday morning; she found a small down-at-heel café finally, had a cup of tea, and then started to walk back home. It was early evening by now, but the day had been fine and she walked briskly, crossed Park

Lane and went the length of South Audley Street into
Grosvenor Square, turned into Duke Street and then
Wigmore Street. There weren't many people about; it
was too late for the sightseers and too early for the theatre
traffic to have started. She got to the flat nicely tired, to
be greeted by Nelson who wanted his supper. She might
as well have her own, she decided, and go to bed early.
Tomorrow she would walk through St James's Park and
into Green Park and in the evening try to go to church.
She could have phoned Doreen, she supposed, but
Doreen didn't like to be rung up on duty, and when Meg
had called her earlier in the week she had said that she
simply hadn't the time to see her. Next week, she
suggested vaguely. And Cora was away, spending the
weekend with her in-laws.

It was raining when she got up in the morning, but the
prospect of a whole day indoors didn't appeal. Meg put
on her raincoat, tied a scarf over her head, and went to St
James's Park where she walked for an hour or more,
stopping to have coffee at a stall before crossing Green
Park into Mayfair and so finally back to the consulting
rooms. She had sandwiches for lunch, sitting before the
fire reading the Sunday papers with Nelson on her knee,
and in the afternoon for something to do, she turned out
the kitchen.

She took more trouble than usual over cooking her
supper; it took time to grill the small trout and make
pepper sauce, cream the potatoes and make a hot fennel
salad, and also just as long to cook the *crème au chocolat*.
Such a waste of time, she reflected, laying the table with
as much care as if she had guests. But it kept her
occupied; she wasn't a girl to cook something out of a tin
and eat it off a tray in front of the television.

She had finished her supper and was trying to decide
whether to go to bed with a book or get on with her

knitting when Doreen phoned.

'A party, love!' she cried loudly into Meg's ear. 'Next Tuesday, and you simply must come! You'll meet masses of new people and it'll be such fun. Half past eight, and wear something pretty.' Before Meg could say a word, she added breathlessly, 'Must go—see you Tuesday.'

It would be something to do, thought Meg, getting into bed; she didn't want to meet masses of people, but she had the good sense to know that to sit at home and brood over the Professor was going to do no good at all.

She got out of bed, causing Nelson, already asleep on her feet, to grumble under his breath, and went to inspect her wardrobe. The black pleated crêpe-de-Chine skirt—she had had it for years but it didn't seem to date—and the oyster satin blouse which she had hardly worn. Not in the least exciting, but she would have no chance to buy anything before Tuesday, and no one was likely to give her more than a casual glance.

She could, of course, have worn the pink, but on reflection, she did decide that she never wanted to wear it again.

Monday was busy, and she had only a glimpse of the Professor arriving in the morning and leaving again in the evening, and on Tuesday he was at the hospital all day. She had her supper as usual, changed into the blouse and skirt, covered them with her winter coat since it was a chilly evening, and took the bus to her sister's hospital. Her flat was five minutes' walk away, and she had been told exactly where to go. It was in a modern block of flats on a pleasant enough street, and easy to find. Meg climbed the stairs to the third floor, and since the door was ajar she walked in. There was a good deal of noise coming from the room at the end of the hall, and an open door on her left revealed a pile of coats on chairs and the bed. She added hers to the pile and went to join the party.

The room was packed with people, and a splendid mixture they were too. The girls were dressed either in tight skirts with slits at the back and vivid silk tops or in rather peculiar loose draperies swathed in layers around them. The men too seemed equally varied: jeans and T-shirts, velvet jackets and pink shirts, one or two nicely cut dark suits and two young men in black leather. Meg stood just inside the door; she had no idea that Doreen was so modern, and knew instantly that her own clothes were, in such company, quite freakish. She caught a glimpse of her sister's handsome head at the end of the room and edged her way round to her.

Doreen was talking to several people and she didn't see Meg at once. She was wearing a slinky black dress with a cascade of beads round her neck, and anyone less like a Ward Sister was hard to imagine. Her eyes lighted on Meg eventually and she cried, 'Darling, there you are! Come and meet everyone!' She cast a worried look at the blouse and skirt, which Meg caught, but covered it at once with a smile. 'This is Tom—he's the surgical registrar—and this is Ned, he's one of the house physicians, and this is Marlene, she's a Theatre Sister . . .'

Meg shook hands and smiled as Doreen led her round the room and then, with a nod and a smile, left her. The small group who had been interrupted by Doreen smiled and said hello and went on talking together, pausing after a moment to ask her which hospital she was from.

'I'm not a nurse,' said Meg. 'I'm Doreen's sister.'

They smiled vaguely and presently drifted away. She wasn't alone for long; a youngish man, one of the T-shirt brigade, flung an arm round her shoulders. 'Hello, darling—all alone?' He studied her at some length. 'In fancy dress, are you? Or someone's nanny?'

'I'm Doreen's sister, and take your arm away, please.'

'Someone's nanny. This isn't quite your scene, is it, darling? What about a ride around and a drink somewhere quiet?'

They were hemmed in by uninterested people's backs. Meg tried to see where Doreen was by standing on tiptoe and peering round shoulders, all the time aware of the man's heavy arm. She was quite capable of squirming away from him, but for all she knew he might be a firm friend of Doreen's from the hospital; besides, one or two people had turned to look at her and were beginning to laugh—the young man's voice carried . . .

Then at the other side of the room the door opened and the Professor walked in.

He stood for a moment, looking about him, oblivious of the interest he had stirred up. Doreen abandoned the people she was talking to and went to meet him. Meg was too far away to hear what she was saying, but the Professor listened gravely, smiled and said something in his turn. If only he'd look this way, thought Meg. She could have spoken out loud, for he looked across the packed room and smiled faintly, said something else to Doreen and made his way towards her.

There was no need for her to say anything; her eyes told him everything. He said easily, 'Hello, there you are—if you're ready, we'll go.'

He took the young man's arm from her shoulder and took her hand.

'I say . . . hang on,' began the young man sullenly.

The Professor ignored him, tucked Meg's hand in his and made a leisurely progress to the door where Doreen was still standing. 'You'll forgive us if we leave? I should have telephoned to say that I wouldn't be able to come this evening, but as I was coming this way to an appointment I thought I'd call in.' He added smoothly, 'I'll see Meg home—I'll be going past the door.'

He barely gave Meg time to bid her sister a bewildered goodbye. In the hall he nodded to the open bedroom door. 'Your coat is there. Put it on, Meg and we'll go.'

Going down the stairs she exclaimed, 'I've only just come!'

He halted so abruptly that she almost overbalanced. 'You would like to go back? I could have sworn that you wanted me to rescue you . . .'

She looked up at his face. 'Oh, I did! I hated it—you see, I didn't look like any of the girls—that man—he asked me if I was in fancy dress and he thought I was someone's nanny.'

Her voice had become a little squeaky despite her best efforts.

The Professor's voice was casual in the extreme. 'My dear girl, you don't give credence to such hubris?'

'What's hubris?'

He laughed. 'Insolence, arrogance, cockiness—any of those.' He went on down the stairs, taking her with him. 'I promise you that you are dressed very nicely, and anything less like a nanny I have yet to meet.'

The very carelessness of his voice reassured her. 'I didn't know you'd been invited,' she remarked.

He didn't answer her but took her arm and marched her out of the house and across the pavement to the Rolls.

'There's a bus . . .'

He opened the car door and ushered her in. Getting in beside her, he said, 'Will you come and have a meal, Meg, I'm famished?'

'You have an appointment—you told Doreen . . .'

'A social lie. I hate eating alone.'

She found it impossible to say no, and anyway he didn't wait for her to answer; he was already driving away from the flat. He took her to the Capital Hotel Restaurant where she found, to her relief, that the other women were dressed with a quiet elegance with which her own appearance merged easily. She heaved a sigh of relief as they sat down at their table, and the Professor hid a smile.

'Champagne, I think,' he observed with an impersonal friendliness she found comforting. 'Now, what shall we eat? The sardines with mustard sauce are excellent, and I can recommend the *caneton Père Léon* ...'

Meg sipped her champagne and was lulled into peaceful content by her companion's gentle flow of talk. They were served with champagne sorbets before the main course and her eyes grew round with delight. Pressed to try the sherry trifle, she did so, and over it, her tongue loosened by the champagne, she talked and laughed as though he were an old friend. It wasn't until much later, when she was back in the flat getting ready for bed, that she recalled this—and still more vivid was the remembrance of his kiss. He had gone up to the flat with her, opened the door and switched on the light, and when she had thanked him for her lovely evening, he had caught her close and kissed her soundly and she had kissed him back, alight with the false euphoria engendered by the champagne and the delight of his company.

Her last waking thought as she fell into a troubled sleep was that she would never be able to face him in the morning.

Of course, she did, sitting self-effacing behind her desk, and his good morning was the usual coolly pleasant greeting without a flicker of warmth.

When the last of the morning's patients had gone, he put his head round the door on his way to the hospital.

'You'll be glad to know that the Pitts have settled in well and the baby's fine. Lucky spends a lot of time with them and they like him.'

Meg felt tears crowding her throat. No self-pity, she

told herself sternly, and managed to say, 'How nice, I'm so glad.'

'I knew you would be.' His voice was silky. When he had gone, she applied herself to tidying her desk and getting out the notes concerning the afternoon's patients. She was a fool to love anyone as unpleasant as the Professor. Not always unpleasant, she corrected herself, thinking of the previous evening.

The weekend came round once more and since it was dry even if overcast, Meg took herself off to Hampton Court, where she did everything the guide book suggested and then took the bus home again, warning Percy when she got in so that the phone could be switched through to her flat once more.

She was cooking her supper when it rang, and she went to answer it. She had a list of numbers where the Professor might be found in an emergency and, sensing the urgency of the voice from Maud's, promised instant help and started systematically on the numbers. His home first, although she thought that Maud's would already have phoned there. Rosie answered, 'He's been out of the house since tea time. Said you had the phone numbers if he was wanted.'

Meg went on down the list, chafing at the small delays while the phone was answered. It was her fourth call before she had success.

She recognised the voice which answered her—the girl. It was a London number, so he wasn't too far away, she thought thankfully, and when the girl said she would give him a message she insisted on speaking to him.

'Culver,' said the Professor in her ear. 'Who wants me, Meg?'

'Maud's. He said it was urgent and I told him that if I could find you you'd phone him. A Mr Wyatt.'

'My registrar. Thanks.' He hung up.

The girl would be furious, thought Meg naughtily.

She had just finished writing to Betsy when the doorbell rang. It was a bit late for anyone to call, but it could be Percy with an offer to empty her kitchen bin. She opened the door on the chain and the Professor said testily, 'Why the caution? You might have guessed it would be me.'

She opened the door and he went past her. 'No, I didn't guess, and it was you who told me never to answer the door unless the chain was up.' She added severely, 'There's no pleasing you, Professor.'

He muttered something and she asked politely, 'Would you like a cup of tea? I've just made some.'

'Tea? At this hour? Yes, yes, I'll have a cup.'

He sat himself down, and Nelson scrambled on to his knee in an elderly fashion.

Meg brought him the tea and offered him a biscuit and they sat munching their digestives, saying nothing, looking at each other. But presently the Professor said, 'I don't understand why you've disrupted my life—you're never the same girl for more than half an hour at a time! You scold me and infuriate me by turns and yet you're a splendid listener. You efface yourself so completely at times that I miss you, and yet you have the gall to foist stray animals into my household. Something must be done about it.

He finished his tea, and Meg said in a matter-of-fact voice, 'Would you like another cup?'

'You see what I mean? I think you've not heard a word of what I've been saying, or worse, you heard it all and chose to ignore it?' He added bleakly. 'My life has always been an ordered one, but that's no longer the case.'

Meg didn't say anything. To a certain extent she had succeeded. At least he had noticed her—it was a pity that he didn't seem very pleased about that. All the same, it was something. She studied his frowning face, loving every line of it.

When the silence had been going on for too long she said kindly, 'You've been working too hard. Can you not take a holiday? I mean a real one, not lectures and things.'

'And now you presume to tell me what I am to do . . .'

'That's rubbish!' said Meg vigorously. 'You know as well as I do that you do exactly what you want. Why did you come here, Professor?'

'Do you know why they wanted me at Maud's this evening?' and when she shook her head, 'Nancy—you remember her? She collapsed. She's all right now; with luck she'll respond to treatment and in a little while she'll be able to go home. She'll have to come into hospital from time to time, but if we can keep her going . . .'

'You will,' said Meg firmly. 'It's a challenge, isn't it?'

He smiled with great charm and she smiled back, quite forgetting to be self-effacing.

'I'm going to Much Hadham tomorrow morning; would you like a lift to see Betsy? I'll pick you up again after tea.'

Her whole face lit up, but she said, 'That is kind of you, but it might not suit your mother.'

'She's lunching with me.' He got to his feet and put Nelson back in his box. 'I'll collect you about ten o'clock.' At the door he said, 'Thanks for the tea. Goodnight, Meg.'

This time he didn't kiss her.

Meg was ready and waiting in the morning; it would be a dull day for Nelson and she wondered if she should take him in his basket, a suggestion to which the Professor instantly agreed. Nelson wasn't a cat to run away, nor was he likely to fight with Silky; he was popped into his basket and settled on the back seat of the Rolls.

The Professor had little to say as he drove; Meg admired the countryside once they reached it, thanked him gravely when they arrived at her old home, spent a few minutes talking to Mrs Culver and went along to the kitchen, where she found Betsy waiting for her. Kate had gone to London to spend the day with a niece and they had the house to themselves. Meg was hugged and kissed and told to sit down while Betsy saw Mrs Culver safely into her son's car.

They spent the morning having a good gossip over their coffee while Nelson and Silky sat in armed neutrality before the stove. Betsy was happy; she liked Kate and Kate liked her, and between them they ran the house with the aid of Mrs Griffiths. The boy who came to see to the garden did outside jobs for them and there was always Noakes, willing to lend a hand. 'A bed of roses, Miss Meg, that's what it is! If you was here it 'ud be perfect.'

'We've both been lucky,' said Meg. 'I like my job and I've got the dearest little flat.'

'Do you see much of Miss Doreen or Miss Cora?'

'Well, they're both so busy ... I went to a party at Doreen's new flat. She has a lot of friends ...'

'You never was one for parties,' declared Betsy. 'Lucky you've got that nice little lodge to go to at weekends.'

'Yes, isn't it?' Meg spoke cheerfully; she had no intention of telling her devoted friend that that was all finished and done with.

She set the table while Betsy saw to their lunch and afterwards when they had washed up and Betsy had gone for what she described as 'a bit of a lay down', she went to the garden and roamed happily. The boy had worked well. As well as the flower borders, the kitchen garden was laid out in orderly rows. Meg went round identifying the green shoots, nodding happily. For a moment she allowed her thoughts to dwell on the little lodge garden. Her careful weekend gardening would be paying dividends now; the tiny grass patch in the centre would be just large enough to hold a pram. She siged and went back into the house and put the kettle on for tea.

It was the kind of tea she seldom had. Betsy was old-fashioned; when Meg's parents had been alive, tea had been sandwiches cut wafer-thin, thin bread and butter and a cake to cut at, and the dear soul had never changed the pleasant habit. Kate, she told Meg, had the same views, so that Mrs Culver, even when alone, was served with some dainty little meal. The kitchen was pleasantly warm, the cats were already asleep, back to back, and Betsy, nicely rested, was inclined to be even chattier than usual.

'It's time Miss Doreen got herself married,' she observed, 'and isn't it about time you found yourself a husband, Miss Meg?' She looked worried. 'Though I suppose the Professor will keep you on after he's married. No call to give you the push when all's said and done. Mrs Culver told me she's delighted that he's found himself a wife—very choosy, he's been, according to her.'

The delicious fruit cake Meg was eating suddenly tasted like sawdust in her mouth. She asked casually, 'I wonder if it's the girl I've seen over at Much Hadham—fair-haired and so pretty ...'

'No idea, Miss Meg. Mrs Culver didn't say. Why not ask him?'

'I'm not all that interested,' said Meg mendaciously.

There was plenty of opportunity to ask him on their way back to London presently. He was in a good mood; he was never a talkative man, but now he had quite a lot to say about the Pitts. The baby was thriving and they were very happy. Pitt was proving a good worker, and Mrs Pitt was willing to help out up at the house if she was needed. 'It's all worked out splendidly!' observed the Professor, glancing sideways at Meg. 'You found Betsy well?'

He carried Nelson's basket up to the flat when they reached it, but beyond switching on the light and taking a quick look round, he didn't stay, but made some bracing remark about the busy morning which lay ahead of them, wished her good night and went away again.

Beyond a rather cross phone call from Doreen during the week, who declared that she had been disagreeably surprised at the way Meg had rushed away from her party and taken the Professor with her, and an equally cross one from Cora whose au pair had left without giving notice, the week went well. 'If you hadn't got this job,' Cora had grumbled, 'you could have come here. Why you had to go off like that I'll never know. Doreen and I would have got you settled in a good job . . .'

Minding Cora's children, thought Meg. 'I'm sorry about the au pair,' she had said, 'but I'm sure you'll find someone. And this is a good job, you know; besides, the flat is lovely . . .'

For how long? she wondered as she rang off. The Professor had said nothing to give her cause for alarm, but she wasn't happy about the future.

'I'm getting fanciful,' she told Nelson. 'I'm not sure that being in love is all that it's cracked up to be.'

She had reason to remember those words that very afternoon.

There were no patients until four o'clock; Miss Standish was taking a couple of hours off and Mrs Giles wouldn't be in until later. Meg, tidying patients' cards in the filing cabinet, heard the Rolls, and a moment later the Professor walked in. He nodded as he crossed to his door and closed it gently behind him, and five minutes later called her over the intercom to go in.

She switched the phone through in case of urgent calls, knocked on the door and stood waiting. She had gone rather pale and she didn't smile as she took the chair he offered her without speaking.

The Professor didn't sit down but came round to lean against his desk, watching her. He said, 'Why do you look like that? As though I were going to sack you?'

Meg clasped her hands in her lap to keep them from shaking. Her insides were filled with an icy foreboding. 'I expect I look like that because you are, aren't you? Going to sack me?'

She peeped up at him and was affronted to see that he was smiling, although he said gravely enough, 'Yes, I am; a Mrs Loftus will be starting on Monday.' And when she was silent, 'Don't you want to know why I want you to leave?'

It was a pity that she had her eyes lowered because she couldn't bear to see him smiling; she missed the look on his face, a look which would have sent her straight into his arms. When she did look it was too late; the phone was ringing and he was answering it.

'Culver.' He listened intently, giving no sign of annoyance because he had been interrupted. 'My dear fellow—this is her second day—does she not understand that she has three more days to go? I thought I'd made it clear that she must remain supine for that length of time.'

He listened again. 'Oh, we can't have that,' he observed. 'I'll come over at once; she'll have to be sedated.' He put down the receiver.

'Later,' he said to Meg as he went through the door.

He got back just after four o'clock, and Meg, who had been keeping his first patient happy with tea and gentle gossip, ushered her in. She was still pale, but no one looking at her composed face would have guessed at her shattered heart.

The second patient came and went, and Mrs Giles and Miss Standish, instead of staying for their usual little chat, went too. Meg tidied up once more and checked the list of patients for the morning, and when the Professor put his head round the door and said, 'Come in, please, Meg,' she did so.

He closed the door and stood leaning against it. 'Now, where were we?' he asked affably.

'You'd just sacked me.'

'Ah, yes—and you've probably spent the last hour or two wondering why?'

She said in an expressionless voice, 'Yes, of course I have. I think it's because I vex you sometimes in some way—I *have* tried not to . . .'

She didn't quite suppress a watery sniff; all her silly, pathetic ideas about attracting his attention were so much moonshine.

'You've never vexed me.' He had left the door and was standing very close to her, looking down on to her neat, downbent head. 'You intrigue me, humble me, delight me, you've wormed your small person into my very heart, but never once have you vexed me. My dearest little darling, I've been in love with you since we first met, although I didn't know it then; I only knew that when you weren't here I missed you intolerably. I'll never be happy until you're my wife.'

He caught her close and held her gently. 'You're so beautiful and kind and loving. I love the way you laugh and grub in the garden and collect stray animals. Darling, would you consider collecting me?'

Meg looked up into his face and saw so much love there that she blinked. 'Oh yes, indeed I will—I can't think of anything I'd rather do!' She smiled radiantly at him. 'I love you, too . . .'

She wasn't given the chance to say more than that. He had kissed her before, but never like this. Presently she sighed happily and caught her breath. 'There are several things . . .' she began, remembering the girl with the golden hair.

'Not important.' He kissed her again.

'Yes, well . . . What shall we do, Ralph?'

'Why not go upstairs and tell Nelson, dear heart?'

'Yes, but what about . . .'

He kissed her quiet. 'Later—I've other plans for the moment.'

'Oh, well,' said Meg happily, 'if you say so.' She reached up and kissed him.

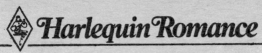
◈ Harlequin Romance

Coming Next Month

2857 A MAN OF CONTRASTS Claudia Jameson
All signs point to a successful union when business owner
Elaine marries a widower with a small son. When she becomes
convinced he's still in love with his first wife, she faces the
future with dismay!

2858 KING OF THE HILL Emma Goldrick
Marcie regards the Adirondacks mountain cabin she inherited
as a needed resting place, until she becomes involved in a
family feud started by her late uncle. Even worse, she fights
with the one man she could love.

2859 VOYAGE OF DISCOVERY Hilda Nickson
Tha Canary Islands cruise is a new experience for Gail—a
pleasant shipboard romance would top it off. But falling in
love is a waste of time when the man in mind is not only
uninterested but engaged!

2860 THE LOVE ARTIST Valerie Parv
Carrie sees famous cartoonist Roger as fancy-free and
irresponsible, just like her father, who'd abandoned his family
to pursue art. No way will she consider Roger as a husband.

2861 RELATIVE STRANGERS Jessica Steele
Zarah travels to Norway to unravel the mystery surrounding
her real mother. She is shocked when she is regarded as a gold
digger even by the one man she can turn to for help—and love.

2862 LOVE UPON THE WIND Sally Stewart
Jenny's quiet London life is disrupted when her lawyer boss's
divorced son asks her to be his secretary. His second request is
even more shattering—to be the wife he needs as a respectable
candidate for Parliament!

Available in August wherever paperback books are sold, or
through Harlequin Reader Service.

In the U.S.
901 Fuhrmann Blvd.
P.O. Box 1397
Buffalo, N.Y. 14240-1397

In Canada
P.O. Box 603
Fort Erie, Ontario
L2A 5X3

Sarah

MAURA SEGER

Sarah wanted desperately to escape the clutches of her cruel father.
Philip needed a mother for his son, a mistress for his plantation.
It was a marriage of convenience.
Then it happened. The love they had tried to deny suddenly became a
blissful reality... only to be challenged by life's hardships and brutal
misfortunes.

In August
Harlequin celebrates

The **1000**th

Presents

Passionate Relationship

by
Penny Jordan

Harlequin Presents,
still and always the No. 1 romance
series in the world!

Available wherever paperback books are sold.

PR1000